MW01689706

Giving Form to Air

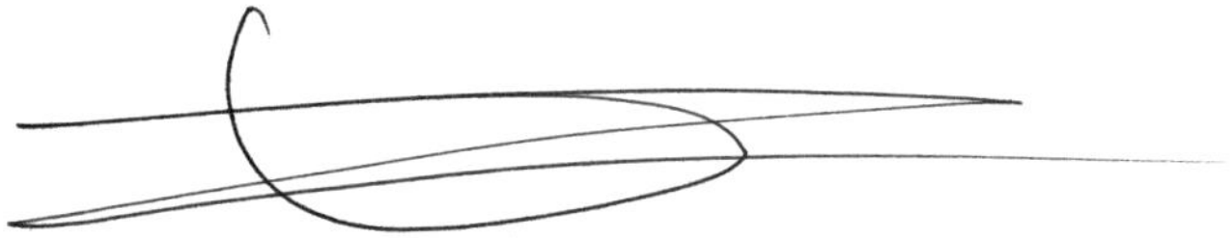

Giving Form to Air

Lyan Alsabti

Copyright © by Lyan Alsabti

All rights reserved. No part of this publication may be reproduced in any manner whatsoever without the prior permission of the publisher, except in the case of brief quotations embodied in critical reviews and certain other noncommercial uses permitted by copyright law.

ISBN: 0-692-19757-5

First paperback edition, October 2018

This is a work of fiction. Names, characters, places, and incidents either are the product of the author's imagination or are used fictitiously. Any resemblance to actual persons, living or dead, events, or locales is entirely coincidental.

Typeset in Questa and Times New Roman

Cover designed by Elijah Wilborn and the author
Cover photograph copyright © Elijah Wilborn

Published with Kindle Direct Publishing

Thank you God,

Mom, Dad, and Sam.

"We are hypnotized by artifice upon artifice, yet yearn for the truth."
–Elon Rutberg via Twitter; April 11, 2017

"The term pro forma *(Latin for "as a matter of form" or "for the sake of form") is most often used to describe a practice or document that is provided as a courtesy or satisfies minimum requirements, conforms to a norm or doctrine, tends to be performed perfunctorily or is considered a formality."*
–Wikipedia

Chapter 1

Heavy bass.

The main workers bounced around the table, stretching their hands out at each other. They tossed oblong high-fives once the climb after the lowest drum hit. These hands occasionally made signs hard for Maralyn to discern, showing off the unblemished backs of their index fingers and thumbs.

Snarling with the teeth showing. Four billion years of organisms only to have them shake around the vibrating floor. Highs and lows; all highs. No suffering. 20 million characters in the code. And the kids were set free.

"I didn't even know how to make a song!" Trevor exclaimed while giggling.

The extra fat at her sides, or her random facial hair, the physical details, could be disregarded in the light of creation.

Again. The high-pitched vocals that normally sprinkled the production suddenly blasted when the hook's 808s resurfaced. Jesse was were a shocking phantom, almost mocking listeners. It was bum, do, do do do, baht! The intense moment repeated twice more, and their distorted guitar came into the foreground. The song would revert to its fast pattern of high-pitched ups and gentle downs.

Brett had shown the formerly rock-only fan Trevor how to, illegally, download FL Studio. And their group now adored the possibilities which they saw in front of them.

Alongside Brett, Sage, Jesse, and a few miscellaneous kids, Maralyn realized that this experience was indiscriminate, not belonging to one type. Still, she was glad that she knew how to thank, who to thank, never overstepping her boundaries. Whoever was even watching, she understood that her identity was on the path of many other sunflower and concrete ones.

With this nuanced vantage point, that ethnicity and skin color; Arab; not white, not black. Maralyn thought: I never realized I could do this,

Thousands of graves throughout thousands of years made it so that the present would happen. Trevor's guitar interpolated through each moment, formulating oblong and perfect layers. His red electric guitar being present on the track felt oddly meaningful to Maralyn. Special, homey, loving, connective. As well as dangerous, rebellious, dirty.

Those rhythms, plus the Jesse's airy vocal melodies, were 100 percent serene. Nobody even understood what Jesse spoke inside Trevor's make-shift closet booth, and they still did not as it played back. But it was good; her heightened and absurd femininity made fire. And there they were, to catch it, record the algorithms for which to replicate it in the future.

The room smelled of high-quality, fresh marijuana. And men's deodorant and expensive perfume. Katrina was (still) invited, but didn't' show up–so nobody felt guilty reveling in the novel activities. But, they all knew, the night would have felt even better with her there.

"I feel like there's something missing," Brett mumbled.

Everybody agreed with that.

It's some piano, I think–Maralyn wanted to reply.

But the boys were already in an excited and distraught frenzy. The style of their conversation excluded her almost automatically. They nitpicked details in the song on their own.

The group collectively decided to add a hushed wind howling sound, found from YouTube. And then, near the track's end, a few gunshots, to repeat after the low drums. The sound effect was chilling, especially in contrast with the vocals and the kids' current setting.

Brett began to bop his head, sparking interest from Maralyn. She began to pace, nearly sweating herself out. Pausing, she stared at the ground and smiled, her eyebrow hoods acting as protection for her transforming inner self.

The trees parted for their happiness; all of theirs–the youth got to shine and stand atop the hill. Every hill, every mountain, and then every little body holding hands.

Boom, daht, daht, daht, daht!

A random line of energy came into Maralyn's mind at one point, it was: *I started to notice the rain*.

Leaving that night, Trevor asked himself: what am I gonna do now?

But a billboard advertisement zipping past Brett and him in Trevor's car, glancing with their refreshed eyes, stated, "WAKE UP"

So, he determined that he should probably do so.

Maralyn had left via her mother–making the tired woman rush so that she could spend out the rest of the inspiration. Simply in her room. She would ignore food, Elias, even her speakers.

Fresh ideas, non-looping visions, would choke her up with love. Done to all of them, all of her acquaintances, everyone there.

But, with the substances, it was hard to discern details.

I feel trapped in my consciousness.

A constant, consistent buzzing sound.

I Don't Know Where To Put These Thoughts

On forever.

Writing things on a box. Fragile, brown box. Like, one that you can buy from the office supplies store and fold when you get home.

It's on.

The TV show. TV screen.

Lapses.

Thundercat's angelic humming and basslines streamed through the speaker. They truly streamed.

Her Tumblr dashboard was open on Maralyn's desktop. A long post with six imaged and a paragraph caption was the second item. It told a story about anti-homophobia protestors from the 1930s. They truly streamed.

Bang, bang, bang!

Somebody slammed on Maralyn's door. She had been in a daze up until then, thinking about the movies an indie rapper recommended on Twitter, while rapidly scrolling through the website. A dizzy shake of the head followed and she got up to open the door. She did so with a confident tiredness.

"Welcome to my room" Maralyn told them, without looking up.

"Dude!" Josiah screamed. He seemed excited about something.

"What," she answered him.

"Did you hear that new Kendrick Lamar?"

If "omg" could be facially expressed, he was making that face.

But before becoming interested in playing it, she paused. Hearing a series of opaque, muffled electricities in her mind.

Chapter 2

War

Ah-errr. Chick chick chick chick, ting! Buhhhmmm.
Buhhmm. Bwhummm. Shooooooh.

"Lucifer Sansfoi
Varlet Sansfoi"
–Jack Kerouac - "A Curse at the Devil"

He awoke to the sound of meerkats squeaking in droves as they located food in their environment. The little boy was seven nearing eight as of this month, and nothing could separate him from the fun childhood activities which he loved. How many moments had gone by?

Then. Powerful flashes of light pressed against his shut eyes. In this microcosm: the field was torn up by a cruel tornado. It had been hard to gauge, using the rectangular forecast, who would be okay and would be not. The boy turned his face from the lanky man smoking a cigarette.

A static-y woman's voice flowed out, saying in an almost sing-songy voice:

"You always meant the world to me
Do you know what you're doing now?"

It transmitted right towards his face, almost.

The boy had his favorite orange cap on–it had a logo from the state baseball team stitched onto the front. The noise of his dad working on kitchen maintenance could be heard from the delicate spot. The boy was seated on the floor now, cross legged in the middle of the oval rug, paying much of his attention to the rectangle ahead. The rug had mainly blue and turquoise shapes and black lines in it. You always meant the world to me. The last of the line rung around in his little head. His little hat had a stitched tag on the back which was reflective. It was grey and said "Made with all organic cotton." And underneath: "100% American"–plus some illegible tiny print on the bottom, reading what seemed to be: TH IS O FOR DOW N .

Close Your Eyes and Remember It

On Level C, the main floor. In the earliest days, there was nobody here but them, and the older kids who eventually went off in their own ways. They were turning in field trip payments together today.

"Your thoughts match with mine." Jay thought as he stepped aside for Maralyn. When she looked up from her counselor forms, a laminated poser faced her. It was on a white brick column. She glared at it for a moment, then hazily thought: This is pointless. My thoughts have been like puzzle pieces lately.

These emotions were clear, like a barely used hotel hot tub or a blinding winter sun. They also sent out a presence of discomfort in the air. Only someone standing close to her could sense it. Only Josiah, Jay for short, really knew how to read the girl and her soul. Only that closest one could put two sides of the equation together. And he only, effortlessly and faster than a calculator, locate her mental issues. And solve.

"Let's move away from here," Jay softly said.

Maralyn looked right into his face. Her face flushed with relief. The pair walked out to leave, towards the main doors during sundown. They always avoided the third floor, aka Floor A, where Sigma kids quietly, safely roamed after school. They moved past forms slowly dying before reaching the door. They both felt safe at the prospect of taking a relaxing drive in Josiah's honey colored car. Maralyn would fantasize about cigarettes. Josiah would never let her smoke them, if she could even acquire them. The seats would smell like after-candle warmness. They were both 16, 11th graders.

Friendship follows us everywhere. Jay thought.

And the boy opened wide the dark green door. The sun was fully bright, although isolated because of this. Nature was preparing itself for its next summer cascade. It rarely heard other voices yet never gave up on its sounds. The concrete contained long cracks, some deep and some sprouting green weeds. The ground was scheduled for construction in June when students no longer convened or rushed into and out of there. There were multiple lots, many schools, many cars, as well as entranceways. This one was the group and its associates' favorite. They entered his vehicle. It was warm, familiar, safe, as expected; they commenced on their way to Maralyn's house.

Twenty-five minutes later (her house was 8 minutes away from the school but he drove slow as they chose songs to play), she removed her mud-crusted low-top Converses with her heel and headed inside. Her brother Elias had the show *House of Cards* blasting in the living room.

The next day.

°RIP to all my idols° Dakota had captioned on Instagram beneath a photo of his cream Vans and right arm holding a venti Dunkin Donuts iced coffee–against wet pavement, a brown plastic bag nearby.

The kids, they'd be there until 1am or their lungs grew too weary, and then flop onto their beds staying there for 15 hours. Most of them were healthy and didn't look like emaciated heroin addicts; they didn't turn down fast food munchies (at least when alone). Henry felt like Clint Eastwood, for some reason, when he logged onto Twitter. Not because of the rogueness and complete isolation from all things Internet, but because he understood a sense of wild yet trustworthy exploration. That artists like him were madly in love with; Jack Kerouac, Miles Davis. They had invited him to their perfumed and lively hangout, via text, and actually kind of late. He remained relaxing on his bed, then eighteen minutes passed before Jesse called him sounding like in a panicky rush.

"What are you doing?" she stammered then, out of breath. "Katrina and Maralyn are here, what are you doing come over,"

"I am sitting here. What do you want?" his voice nasally.

"Just come through," and she hung up, Henry catching excited, high-pitched shouts in the background.

So he was here. And Dakota and Rosie were cuddling Heather's couch, King Krule was playing, the room smelled like McDonald's and the flower bouquets. Parents wouldn't be home until 12am because of a work party "or something." The group used this to their advantage fully to blast rap or alternative music and smoke in the backyard. It was mainly cigarettes that day; speaking of which, Katrina needed a new pack.

"Where the fuck can a girl get some Camel Blues out here?" she projected, sitting alone on the other couch and almost possessing it. "Is Brett coming, when is Brett coming?"

Both her and Dakota knew that he could just buy some for her, as he was 18, but she didn't want to bother him. Especially because he was relaxing with Rosie. He gave her an uncomfortable look from the couch.

"You don't need to let her use you again," Rosie muttered in his ear, the last word straying off.

"No, it's okay," he replied at speaking volume.

"Katrina,"

The girl put her phone down and quickly turned to him. "What's up,"

"I mean I can go buy some Camels for you, there's a gas station not far from here,"

And this is where most people stopped paying attention, restoring connection to the tv, their nonsensical discussions, and drug-buying/selling plans. Henry was still enjoying reading recent news article headlines and Internet threads, so he refocused on the device in his hands.

As usual, Maralyn contributed a general air of anxiety. But she was happy, and she thought about family Wal-Mart trips and the possibilities of making well-liked, lasting art. Her eyes kept reverting to Katrina, only her silhouette or movements, yet she experienced a sense of good personal boundaries today.

When an image of her favorite camera appeared in her mind, she thought: Stressed about all this…about our Video and how to use the camera and making it right…hopefully Josiah is *supportive*, I guess,

Maralyn had great skill in video editing software, her favorite was the clean and accessible Adobe Premiere Pro, and creative direction. She liked to think that her and Josiah were a great team, Josiah feeding the musical, lyrical fire and her making scenes and cutting concepts.

Sometimes it was hard for people to listen to her directions, as she was short compared to her mostly European-blooded peers, but she had a thick build and a commanding voice. It was semi-raspy and interesting, an accent striving to be as American as possible. Boys, and girls, generally found her attractive, especially because she clearly paid attention to her curves and miscellaneous fat. Her medium-length brunette hair was wavy and joined thrift store pieces for a simple demeanor.

It wasn't a secret to her close friends that Maralyn was weak to the effects of drugs; she was susceptible to the wrong dealers, the existential anxiety consequences, maybe more unnamed. But as of then, she could handle the physical disorientation and party settings, so she wasn't interested in any big changes.

"Maralyn, do you wanna come with us?" Rosie asked while getting her things ready, taking M out of her daze.

"Oh, sure," She felt worried, and magnetized towards whatever Katrina wanted.

"Okay let's go," Dakota announced, meaning that whoever wanted to go would have to go now. No bullshit, no waiting.

5 of them, Jesse one of them, hopped into Dakota's large silver SUV. Jesse's and Katrina's legs pressed together in the third row–which didn't bother Maralyn but was something she almost couldn't ignore.

The time quickly went by, and most of it was a blur to Maralyn, who was on her phone trying to reach Josiah during the entire car ride and back. It reached 9pm and her mom texted her that she had to come home–she could pick her up. Maralyn could drive but did not have her own car yet, her parents couldn't afford it yet.

She played a Marina and the Diamonds song using the AUX cable in her mom's small Buick. As she nodded her head up and down, in a daze towards the window, her mother brought her into conversation.

"What do you smell like?" she calmly and semi-sarcastically asked.

"Uh," Maralyn immediately responded, then she sank into her seat. She drew on the glass with her index finger, trying to stifle the entire moment.

Her mother simply shook her head. She made an upset and angry face, ignoring Maralyn's eyes for the rest of the night. She was a registered nurse, who had fought for her degree in Iraq, so she had much knowledge to justify her emotions. But it was more like true concern than petty annoyance–something the girl had a difficult time seeing.

Staring so deeply, intently that it seemed like it was staring back.

Just as coldly. Its stainless steel edges reflected images like corneas. And maybe the vital shapes of the machine were its oscillating contents–not the tangible, analog stuff.

After his mother violently screamed to turn it off, it was 4am, he turned it off. He depressedly dragged himself onto his bed, in his room which was 3 doors down.

"This can't be for nothing,
We live for something"
–THEY. - Dante's Creek

"What do you remember about it?" she recalled hearing. From a friend, sometime last week. A dark purple shadow with a white outline was the memory's host. No eyes–or no eyes in view.

I don't know why I'm still doing this, she thought now.

Maybe it was–speaking from a point of hesitation–all just something to impress somebody. But there was secret reassurance in that. Her clearing was crowded with wild plants, weeds, berries, all unidentifiable by Maralyn. What she could always make out there were the empty paths to the parking spots or the other side.

To impress somebody.

The thought rang back at her with no warning. Rarely did she talk to herself, or at least look at herself like someone else was there, but now she self-reacted with raised eyebrows and a turbulent gut.

Normally, thoughts flew out, and people used metaphorical devices with rivers or other water systems to help describe them. Thoughts were at least supposed to flow. Yet the drizzle of her consciousness worked in refrains, beep, going on and off, still enough to wet people on a 12 foot journey from the car to their building. This confusion immobilized her temporarily.

There she was, standing in the middle of the forest with a board-straight and tense back, a hand clutching her phone. Then an airiness began to grow below her, starting with the bottom of the feet. She looked at the aging brown leaves around her, they were with her. They assumed a featherness to them, or maybe this was the hollow bones and clear blood sensation at her legs and radiating upwards.

Well. Oh well,

That summed up her feelings about this solitary predicament. As well as, this is pretty cool,

Checking her phone for the time and not even caring, she hauled on her backpack and straightened up to leave. The last movement seemed like it caused a minor earthquake. She remembered the eyes of middle-aged white men who would glare at her at Starbucks.

Maralyn shoved open the door, then stepped into the car which she could barely drive. She made it to her destination in 13 minutes. At her beige-bricked 3 bedroom home. The square windows in her room were emphasized now, given the moody navy blue curtains against evening light trickling in. There was a peculiar trimmed, white ceiling. Her parents implemented this so that there would be more brightness for studying. It bothered her when she was younger, but the way it piqued compliments made her less embarrassed about it.

The floor was dirty brown rows of wood, still polished to an odd shine. In the middle was a large, oval rug, its tacky purple and white flowers suggesting innocence and safety. The family wasn't concerned about damages to the ground anyways since they planned to pass the estate down to one of the kids in later years. Maralyn would softly rebuke the idea of owning this place one day, but she tried not to think about it too much and displayed appreciation.

Above her desk, sketches and plans for shoots, plots, projects and Projects, goals, inspiration hung. These cut-outs were often wrinkly with age and poor gluing. Some, like the 23.4 x 16.5 photo of Jim Morrison performing, had been up there for years. The quotes and song lyrics were usually on little horizontal strips after being typed out with cool fonts, nestled between the pictures. Newer drawings of video outfits and directions (angles, specific time cues, colored pencil work, arrows) dominated the scene in the middle; messily, some photos overlapping and even hiding details.

In the right corner, Harman Kardon speakers (which she got for Christmas in 10th grade) sat next to a CD player topped with two stacks: CDs and cassettes. She played a cassette in her dad's car in those deep nights feeling the world. A box of KFC biscuits and a large iced tea sat on the table next to her bed. It acted as a nightstand too, where she'd set her iPhone overnight so it could wake her up.

Her little brother's smaller room was down the hall next to their shared bathroom. Their floor was usually quiet, when new songs weren't blasting or hangouts weren't going on; the two were calm, slow-moving, and focused on not being disappointments like most teenagers. In this, they bonded; so did they in the alternative, experimental or even emo playlists one of them usually had going on somewhere. It was common to hear Gerard Way shouting in the bathroom from Elias' portable speaker.

Music was in fact playing from her speakers. At medium volume, Danny Brown's forceful voice rapped the song "Outer Space," the turns of his breaths sounding like near squeaks. The lyrics were absurd, backed by an equally absurd instrumental. But it was all respectable and pitiful; his prickly confusions were ever there. The ups and downs echoed throughout the room, and to the hallway. The phrase "beneath the sea" would repeat in M's head throughout the rest of the evening.

Before she went to sleep, she looked up to the Jim Morrison on her wall. Ignoring the purplish sky backdrop, she admired his facial features and frozen cadence. When she discovered a buildup of spit in her mouth, she calmly swallowed it and attempted to sleep.

There she lay, resting, satiated, not angry. Jim seemed to be lowkey judging her and whatever else could be ascertained from his position in the room. He tried to formulate her world history, her family's opinion of her, her habits good and bad. Maralyn was accepting of it. The transmission of energy between the two could be swift, open, and friendly. This was what she was on and what she wanted. She didn't want to piss off or offend any dead idols, or friends. A feeling of empathy permeated the poster of Jim Morrison from that night forward. Picking her iPhone up for her regular dose of memes, she caught a good one after scrolling for a couple minutes. She typically avoided looking at her pulsating and disorderly profile when trying to relax.

It was a photo of the singer and rapper Drake without any caption, just his face whitened, edited into a female anime character. She locked her phone after a sassy chuckle, deciding that it was truly time for bed. Enough of this sick and beautiful world. Once the light from it was over with, a slight amount of moonlight crept in via the blinds. It hinted at a purple hue, puncturing the swollen grey clouds. Now, human dreams and the greater atmosphere latched onto each other. It promised peace for whoever could swiftly breathe it in and out. After a few heavy breaths, Maralyn was off to sleep.

There stood the ego. And surrounding it in borders were the mind's boundaries.

The self as everything. There was no questioning what the self was, at any point in existence/time. The words were the self.

Purple, feathers, satisfying textures like velvet and suede, and ASMR sounds, these flew about the space where a ceiling fan usually goes.

Guitar riffs, immediate communication through the eyes.

Drunks. There were no intoxicated people around.

School lessons…school. It held a lot of weight in small quantities now, here. Things with a darkened, yet potent, significance.

Maralyn could block off the outside voices. She looked down at her reddish sweaty palms. An affirmation begun, given the material and fleshiness. An inner affirmation, it was. She was thick-skinned. Her figurative heart was made of a confident, brave metal, which also had capabilities to destruct.

There were really no extensions of thoughts now. Maralyn–"Maralyn"–an organism, the most credible, trustworthy, impossibly incredible object in the space. About the current space, well, what was it compared to something warm that could be held in a giant's arms? War existed in the world. Was history or the popular media worthy of the closeness of her stories? The cold, the dead and threatening to die, could not find its way around here.

Murder was laughable. It was an absurdity, forgettable and forgotten after mentioned. But, evil, in the likes of anxiety, lurked deep in the wooden walled basement of her persona. Evil was inevitable, a piece of the balances which determined nature and which were determined by it. The parents left the door to the damp boiler room locked unless repairful examination was necessary. The counter-points to badness and wrongdoing were being entertained by the sparkles which dotted her arms inside of a tunnel of sunlight.

Suddenly hearing her mother downstairs, something took to the forefront of her mind, which made her head not stop spinning, but helped it turn in a more graceful cycle. Regardless, the spin was epic. She was thankful for all the moments where her mom had supported her, and felt flows of comfort as she remembered their beautiful memories together. The standstill allowed her gratitude a full session, as fleeting as it was.

Maralyn's eyes completely shut for a thorough moment of appreciation in truth.

And the truth was love. Love was the truth.

Chapter 3

She awoke 30 minutes before school, mouthwashed instead of brushing, and headed to school alongside Elias.

He had stared at his phone during the entire ride. Their mom dropped them off at the main entrance, but Maralyn quickly scurried around those doors, to her parking lot. She tried to simply forget that her mother muttered "I'm worried about you, Maralyn" before they pulled in.

Her friend group's favorite entrance included elevators which lead to both Sigma and Middleton, but it was mostly the latter students who used it. The lot, with a low concrete roof covering half of it and looming trees, seemed dirty and ancient. Today she had no time to enjoy the dark scenery, so she got straight into the elevator. "B" was pressed and she was off to the library.

There, Jay and Heather both agreed that Maralyn's new dark red sweater was lovely, especially in how it suited her personality. She noticed them staring at her and smirked. They used her response to enter into a new topic.

"Show me your Project Research outline, bro," Heather asked her.

Maralyn would easily oblige because she believed that it was important to help people out in the Non-Creative portions where she could. Those things did not take or give regarding reputation or originality. All students just suffered equally. It seemed, on that wet morning, that only she felt realized this. She sensed some speckles of green envy, possibly, in Josiah's eyes.

Deal with our bullshit! she wanted to yell to the sky for her teachers and administrators to hear. Don't put it all on the rest of us,

"We're writing up outlines on our own, and then finishing the paper somewhere. We're gonna try to combine ideas and add all the research findings and article studies," she described to Heather. "It'll take a little time, just a little, but we'll get it done."

The last part was sarcastic–30 to 35 pages did not take a little bit of time.

The general consensus at Opifer was that the long assignments were irrationally hard to deal with. Or at least inconsiderate of teenage stresses and endeavors. And they could either catapult a student to a new dimension of careers or be labeled a trust fall. "This could really serve as back-up for you if you do well," teachers would say, referencing grades and Creative Projects. They would then run away subtly if this did not happen. It usually did not–colleges did not appreciate good community service alone.

The clear feeling behind a memory came to Maralyn suddenly. It was 10th grade, she was giving her solo presentation in Intro to Government. Mr. Beaman, who became the Principal of Middleton the next year, was the teacher. She writhed as she remembered the glossy, almost dead look in his eyes as she excitedly defended political journalism. She cried out about it to Josiah afterwards, but his response was almost just as blank.

Back to the Projects: most kids (at Middleton in particular) despised how the assignments encouraged volunteerism, but with certain ulterior motives.

The good that could come out, though, and still after physical stamina and good resources, was the high of Project Day.

Soon but long after this morning moment in the library, the friend group would help out with Josiah and Maralyn's Project research. The goal was to get at least 12 different perspectives about the entire school group, especially in relation to one's own current school.

Research papers were required for the semester one (of junior year, usually) Volunteer portion; the actual initiatives were nearly entirely left up to the students to decide. It was an unspoken rule that turning in 15-25 hours of group work in STEM, education, or fixing abandoned houses was sure to get As. Maralyn and Jay's was a social justice mission. In the end, 5 of the write-ups they got back were generally basic, unopinionated summaries of the school's system. Trevor's was included in that and the rest were from lowkey kids who blended in well.

"This damnass, shitty ass school," Josiah proclaimed unforgivingly. Then, he turned his body to face their "audience."

Maralyn nodded. "Describe it," she added. "But maybe not like that."

"Yeah, true. But feel free to write it like that. We'll take care of the editing,"

Jesse began scribbling: "There are seven schools here in total. Two high schools, one is a mix of a middle and high school (with 11 to 18 year olds, specifically), two middle schools, and one elementary school."

She began a new line.

"About 2,100 students go to the school in total. We call it "the school" for ease and convenience, but it's a complex of schools, kind of like a district."

She nodded, thinking: yes–like a school district, in other areas.

"It's called the Opiferum Schoolyard for Excellence. No one in their right minds except news reporters and forms calls it that, we all call it Opifer. The teachers are also supposed to be called Directors but literally no one calls them that, I don't know why they haven't changed it yet."

"The little schools (even though they have hundreds of people) are each staffed differently, yet they are still united by the same "owners" and school board. Some of the schools are "private" and some of them are public. The private ones just have more control on the upper levels, where principals and teachers can make bad decisions and ignore injustices and suffering more easily. Anyways. The President of the entire Opifer complex is David C. Barton. The Vice President (who is retiring soon) is Genevieve something. I can't name any of the other members...

"Usually, people at Triat Middle School go to Middleton and those at Lucida go to Sigma. They go to the second one if they score really well on a test. They're basically endorsed by the school staff to go to it if they also "performed" well in leadership, "creativity", communication, being unique, and things like that. That's the only way a student can attend Sigma. And also, it's slightly upper-class because it's private and expensive. So you also have to be rich. Transfer students also have to meet all of the above, but their GPA is used instead of that test. When you start at elementary school here, which is most students, your middle school is determined by your grades and a group interview with you and your parents. Normally the decision is cut out pretty early on, since the teachers are always watching you and your friends and your grades, even though these things don't mean much as a child. And kids change. That's just my opinion, though."

Her paper was filled with eraser shavings. The kids added and rearranged phrases throughout their narratives. So as to be as accurate as possible, to their knowledge and experiences.

A plane with a darkly buzzing song flew by overhead. The E level room (for meetings, planning, professional development–separated from elementary school classrooms) felt chilly but was set at 71°F. While waiting more than 20 minutes for responses, Josiah took a pencil and decided to lend his own thoughts (which could not count for the paper of course).

He thought: if somebody asked me to describe the cultures of the schools, I would describe Middleton as simple, slightly naive, and caring. It's also very diverse, definitely more so than Sigma. But that's all shallow,

He wrote, "Well, it can be easy to see the differences between them as an outsider, like myself. I moved here in sixth grade, from a small, crappy private school in Connecticut. I went to Triat and now I go to Middleton. I've personally enjoyed my time, and met most of my good friends, but some people don't…"

A few more lines later, he recorded, "Sigma kids, well, I would describe them as kind of entitled. You know, in the way that they walk and talk to their parents and what not (and also how their parents treat them). They're kind of secluded. At least more than Middleton kids. From reality and its hardships, "regular life," it seems like they happily roam around in their own worlds. Oh and the two typically don't "get along," but the more popular kids at each school are all friends with each other, and then the cooler ones of the lot meet and hang out with each other. That's why a lot of people make music or are into fashion and stuff, because it unites people. That's art I guess. All in all, I had a decent experience as a kid, where I met my friends. I think that's all I can truthfully and confidently write about the schools. Our schools."

As for Maralyn, she would formalize her own response in their final research paper. To pass the time, she wrote while smiling, making the others giggle because they knew she was up to something: "Fuck the school. And the schools. Fuck the population. Fuck my life. Fuck your responses. Fuck this paper. Fuck Mrs. Millington. Fuck Opiferum Schoolyard for Excellence. Fuck Mr. Barton. Mr. David C. Barton* I mean. And fuck my ass and my dick and your dick and 69 and life goals and my career and photography and Travis Scott and having friends and rock music and going to concerts and Twitter and Instagram and love and support and truth and happiness and joy and hell, even Mr. Allen. Fuck that guy, hate him. Fuck everybody, for that matter."

At the end of the 25 minutes, Maralyn whipped out her responses and read them aloud.

Heather said, "You know, I think you took it a little too far at the end, but I really appreciated the social commentary located in the first few lines."

Everybody laughed.

"Why thank you very much, bitch." Maralyn replied, and then curtsied.

Everybody was also collectively shaken when somebody knocked the door. They all became silence and paused, waiting for the door to open.

It was Mr. Willis.

"Oh my fucking god," Josiah said under his breath.

They all nervously sighed. They were glad that Rosie and her friend weren't caught vaping in there. Although they knew that Mr. Willis was more lax about that than any other teacher.

"Well hello, group," the teacher announced. "What are you all doing here?"

Their friends looked to Josiah and Maralyn.

After hesitating, Maralyn told him, "Doing Project research."

"Yeah," Jay added.

"Okay, well, we're gonna need this room for a meeting. So get out or feel free to join us,"

Josiah rolled his eyes.

"Yeah okay, sure, we'll leave in a few minutes," she hesitated.

And everybody packed up their things without thinking twice–Rosie and Maralyn glad that they could vape somewhere else in peace. The friends walked out of school together, at their lot, in innocent excitement.

Chapter 4

What Is Your Light?

It was the next day, Saturday. Katrina's house.

Her shoulder blades hung over her head in a near animalistic fashion. She gave it all up, she let loose, then. The light green basin had streaks of toothpaste stuck on it. There were also little rust spots around the surface, and Katrina could see into these details in her position. The hallway still smelled like the apple cider that her mother had made earlier, which was pleasant.

°Is this even important?° Is it meaningful?

She stared herself in the mirror after setting her phone down. Reflected on the girl. The word "short" came to mind; she wasn't sure what it referred to but felt like that knowledge might help her out one day.

While her mom made lots of noise in the kitchen, she thought: I could literally tell Maralyn my dad was dying in a car cash and she'd just look away embarrassed and smile. And she'd say it in her little raspy, nonchalant way. This moment happened while she examined the recently cleaned glass.

What I want is just for her to respect me, and know me, she signed. And to acknowledge me somehow, to acknowledge that I am there,

To be respected with the heart.

I'm not some idea of myself; hey, I'm me. She glared at the mirror. If you love me, don't you have to know that?

She applied a natural lemongrass and almond perfume to her shoulders and scurried out of the bathroom.

The trees in hibernation by the house windows shivered as she passed by them, but they didn't stop for anyone. Her mother was making a true ruckus down the hallway. The tv blasted a kid's show for her baby brother. Katrina rolled her eyes when she caught it, then she reached a strange moment of profound silence. Inner silence. She furrowed her hooded eyebrows once she stepped back into the bathroom, overlooking the counter.

Is this really what I wanted?

"Pshh."

The girl deeply inhaled. When she shifted her weight, her Vans' crunched on something. Somebody's late-night crumbs or a bug or something. Her iPhone suddenly glowed with a notification from the school's gradebook application. The lockscreen showed a time not late for a high school kid but early for Katrina. The chorus of "You Belong With Me" by Taylor Swift became stuck in her head.

God, I love girls, she thought–wondrously, erratically, torturously.

She turned off the lights on her way into the home's darkness.

It is approaching ten p.m. and the set is on. It is ON.

Woah, he thinks, rapidly blinking to make sure that the device and not he was glitching, or maybe just to double-check his realness. Check his status as a child with his merely figurative intellect. And it needs to be reaffirmed.

The box's edges began to shake. Its four sides seemed like they would completely cave in and give up at any time now. If it was a picture frame, the wood's yellow flesh ripped and exposed.

It was falling apart.

"Mom?" said with an American boy's rocky bump on the "o." No nervousness, just disappointment. The unknown. Everything. Fear of the unknown.

His fragile body with soft beige skin is not his mind.

If the screen, everything, broke, would Mom and Dad get him a new one? Mom or Dad, he remembered to remember.

The weekend calmly and chaotically passed. Maralyn quickly poked earphones in on the drive to school, to both stifle her brother's high-pitched complaining and to absorb some early punk rock songs.

People are so pretty, she thought while facing the window.

Their dad said, in a mix of English and Arabic, "So what's up, guys? Want to see a movie bil leil?"

Maralyn smirked at his morning giddiness and language mixture, although she barely heard it. She also didn't see his face when he spoke, it was focused and caring.

"Yeah, Elias? What's up? Wanna see a movie, hoe?"

"Can you shut the fuck up?" he responded, slouched in the front seat.

Their father retorted with a snapping of the tongue and roof of mouth and then, "Ayb! Don't talk to your sister like that."

His name was George Gadiel, someone who took pride as a man that his children were healthy and attending one of the state's most notable high schools.

"Just tell her to stop talking to me. Please and thank you," he said while glued to his phone.

Maralyn Gadiel's smirk persisted.

Her and her father were on happy terms then, because the night before, she spent an hour teaching him how to use Facebook.

He had asked, her name curling, "Maralyn? Can you help me with this computer?"

And when he consistently found adding friends difficult, she told him, "It's just a website; it's nothing bigger than you," "Look, this is how you open a link," "...and how to copy and paste."

The complex trio arrived in ten minutes, to masses rushing in a few minutes before class started.

Chapter 5

It was Wednesday. Fresh organic carrots and massive lettuce leaves lied on the kitchen table. Maralyn's mom would prepare them into the night's appetizers, as her aunt and uncle were coming over. She would awkwardly lend her presence for at least twenty minutes at a time, and her brother would probably be obnoxious after losing his soccer game.

At least he's getting into The Doors, Maralyn thought.

They could listen together once the evening freed up.

She walked into the kitchen during a break from staring at her phone upstairs and comically said hi to her mom.

"Do you want some hummus and pita?" her mother asked.

"Yeah," Maralyn answered weakly. It was only 6, but with her stress it was getting late.

"Good," her mom said. "You can go to bed soon if you want. I hope the noise doesn't bother you,"

"No no, it'll be alright,"

"Okay, habibti. Sit down for now," she answered.

Maralyn found a comfortable spot on the couch for cramming an English article before going back up. She could access class materials with Opifer's official app, probably the most shared benefit of its students. No distinction between class or income level, just an Internet program.

The phone was bright in the girl's face. The mini platter her mom handed over was carefully thought out: baby carrots, cucumber slices, and triangled pita bread surrounding dollops of hummus and laban. She ate mainly from the cucumbers and pita bread, experiencing a precious inner warmth.

Later when it was time to go to bed–the siblings hadn't blasted music after their relatives left–her purple toothbrush seemed abnormal in her right hand. Glaring at its cheap design and ruffled bristles, she felt that pre-sleep consciousness was plaguing her. She washed her face frustratedly, with water only.

Why do people never discuss their nightly routines, or habits? she thought. Like, why do I feel like it's so shameful or embarrassing to talk about pillowcases or who does our laundry or if people even brush in the morning?

She often forgot to brush her teeth the first scheduled time of the day. These cultural rituals. Western, right arrow, American, right arrow. What her companions and her were told growing up.

Maralyn was glad that these ideas were isolated to only herself, for fear of seeming unsanitary. Unusual for an eventful day, she fell asleep without thinking about it.

Then. When she woke up, Maralyn experienced a vague presentiment that the day would be both mysterious and loving.

Somehow–she thought–but the unexpected always happens. Especially in my life,

She did school, arbitrary and irrelevant things happened in her grade school emptiness, then she met with her friends.

They shared a weird moment together. Katrina had snuck half a cigarette in at their lot, Heather and Sage blocking her from sight. Not a full one because that was just too risky. Then, a baby-faced white girl from the Sigma-only entrance began staring at them. She was resting her back on her blocky, overstuffed bookbag on the bench, while apparently waiting for a ride.

Katrina wanted to ask her if she needed one, but was offput by the girl's quizzical, distant glares. She seemed like a kind person to her, but dangerously sheltered. She thought, there's no time for snitches nowadays.

"Anyways," Katrina said in her lowest voice, nonchalant, taking a drag and not looking at anyone.

"How are you *doing*, Katrina," Jesse suddenly asked.

Instead of replying, maybe she hadn't heard it, the girl turned around and stretched her arms out wide. Looking up at the shining clouds, she heaved in physical relief.

Maralyn giggled.

"Heyo," she then said. "Give me a little of that,"

Katrina's head snapped back to the group, her lips still full with drowsy comfort. "What, this?"

"Yes," Maralyn answered nervously, closing her eyes and not even noticing the cigarette being handed to her.

"What?" Katrina told her. "You said you wanted it,"

Jesse and a silent Josiah shifted around, trying to change the

"Um, yeah. Thanks," she replied. "Thank you,"

A New Ga_me.

"You have great character, my friend."

The grave, yet hopeful and reassuring voice, tells the boy. The eyes flash across the screen, surrounded in a turquoise mist. The ultimate visionary of the world is speaking, directly to the audience.

His resonance is a stark, electrical white, differentiated with the room's pitch darkness. No other being is around.

"Be daring, now!" the tall green letters read. There is no symbolism in this green.

Motions begin to momentarily slow down. The boy, his is a state of politeness for this grand teacher and his calm resoluteness in the face of mysterious fate. Endings and conclusions are the same in all modes: in his cushiony seat, through the screen, and in this galaxy. The boy doesn't usually pause to acknowledge the silent transactions.

There's a tiny different between silence and violent solitude.

The small boy's mind dances in oneness. In his vortex, the boy gains some love and peace. They are of mild forms, but so is everything else. There is nothing else. Comparisons and relativity can not exist. Ignoring these bigger questions and releasing them when they arrived. That is how he maintains inner peace.

The longfaced, hurly "wise sage" keeps a superior smirk. His glance seems astounded, at something alien, towards the viewer. It is borderline sad.

Katrina and Maralyn were together once; it ended when Maralyn couldn't muster enough confidence to fit in with her friends and Katrina deleted their Instagram photos together.

irl

The sandalwood candle didn't match her mood, but she still lit it, reclining in her desk chair. Maralyn thought about Kid Cudi. She took out a pencil and her dark green pleather idea journal, writing down things which permeated heavily/spun softly in her mind now.

How could you be the one,
Be the one,
to save me?
To save me?
Frankly

But you are
time,
You are not the time of my life

I don't even know what that means, she thought, then shoved the journal aside.

Maralyn recorded lines which applied directly to her situations, because they were born entirely of them–subconsciously or memorially. It felt like whenever she wrote about Katrina, she never wanted to stop. An image of her new boy's clothing style came to her, and she felt a burst of bitter jealousy. That she wanted to swat away. But it glued to her artistic mind, this creative mind in devotion to her beautiful friend's soul. His loose-fitting dark jeans, Supreme t-shirts, slender piano fingers.

"I once wanted to feel something
But the thought of you is a glue
And I love it.....I love you !!"

I think I love you a lot.
What does that even mean, bro?

Chapter 6

It was Monday evening. Maralyn woke up from her nap. She looked to her left. Her head turned exactly 45°.

There were the eyes. There was the wall.

The sky blue paint did a good job of being real. It seemed as if it was trying to say something. Maralyn's eyes darted to in front of her, then slightly down towards her backpack on the ground. These motions were cutting each other off as they procured into reality, hushed away by the multiple airs of her conscience.

There was something like a little child, who posed as an angel in a capsule of truth, who tried to speak to her now. They sat on the plan wooden floor together. She could not see them. Maralyn did not feel their presence in the moment. But the messenger spoke.

"Be stronger now." she heard. In a tone completely bright, yet rooted in the earth, they spoke it.

Each word was clear and free of memory of the last. The impact of the microspeech began at the wall to her right and encircled Maralyn in finale. Suddenly, the girl put forth discovery within her reach and efforted a decision. The creepy eyes were not right. She remembered the ways in which paranoia acts as a shadow, or mocking blood red curtain, against all forms. Sitting there after those eyes had again lurked into her most private corners, her frustration bordered on true fear, and this led to a good bit of anger.

Her inquisitive spur was partly inspired by this frustration. She let the surprising dismay clear out like a recently unfurled rug. It was on top of that mental layout that she built more ideas, made more sense. The hill sent Maralyn on her way to a higher plane of strength and inner peace. The inspiration which oozed from the build helped to form the words she spoke to others hereafter.

Finesse Beauty

Maralyn stared Katrina in the face as they both crammed math homework. This typically meant copying answers from one another and talking about music or famous cute boys or politics.

Katrina had deep-set hazel eyes, which seemed to be coated in a sweet glaze when she laughed or cried. They were topped off with, or rather accentuated by, well-defined and feminine cheekbones. Her eyebrows, a tint darker than her wavy hair, were golden brown. It matched with her olive skin to create the unique pleasantness of her look, giving off a sort of sweeping and morose, yet deeply courageous energy. She had a darkness to her, and it was nice to look at.

She easily tanned which tended to brighten her skin. And although she didn't like it, her slight brownness softened her personality, especially when her two cheek dimples appeared. Her face was classified as narrow, but it was proportional to her body, getting that from her beautiful mother. Her limbs were elongated, making her look older for her age. Katrina typically showed off a slow sense of being satisfied. Never allowed herself to become overworked by physical tasks, so as to not *reek* or appear ruffled, plus her style always carrying a comfortable, inviting air. Plus she always smelled like new flowers, even walking like one.

Her lips were a point of contestation. Some, boys mainly, thought that were too sculpted, also adding an intimidating layer alongside her point noise. Maralyn thought that they were magical. It never occurred to her that they were even something imperfect to consider. Granted, she might have used an emotional standpoint towards the girl, but she was beyond content with that, with any way that she saw her. Many girls were jealous of Katrina's lips and nose, though. Her looks had the right blend between leaderly tallness and idyllic vitality.

"Dystopias are real. So is hell," Katrina stated lightly yet forwardly.

Maralyn was spacing out.

Then she said, "Us having to go through these things is an example of that."

The half Mexican, half Puerto Rican girl's insecurities had a way of appearing like simply bold calmness. Katrina seemed less aware about it than others, or perhaps she had accepted it long ago and used it to her advantage. The content of her words matched the fragility of her usual tone. In a sense, she was perfectly genuine. And that was what got people far in the realm of sociability, being genuine. It was why deeply-hated, uneducated world leaders got so far in elections and businesses. Because they were themselves and disregarded opinions.

To Maralyn, Katrina's demeanor was hard to ever ignore, but she always tried to stifle the energy. Not fitting in nicely with anyone but herself, especially Maralyn, so not really worth wasting time over. Assumptions worked best here as these people closed themselves off too intensely for anything meaningful. But she felt like boys went wild over girls like that. They loved to protect them and try to get the girls to open up. She thought, that's like her and Trevor, or her and Riley. Riley was Katrina's ex-boyfriend, a year older, into cars and psychedelics.

Although she was bored, M paid close attention after Katrina said, "I'm not trying for my Projects because Mrs. Millington doesn't give a shit anyways if I even show up to class."

It was one of the lengthiest things she had ever heard her say at once. After a few quick minutes, Katrina stood up, packing up what few school things she had.

She ended up leaving to nap. A cigarette first because she *had* to cherish that she was home alone. Maralyn stared at the nothing surrounding her, which was the space left behind by her friend. When she could finally leave too, rushing in her online homework, she tried to have a peaceful rest of the day.

Katrina slept until 7pm, scanning her completely brightened phone before scribbling Project video ideas. She saw a notification from Maralyn, it was on her latest Instagram photo.

"Mon ami est très joli, il semble" it read.

Her head became a woozy. She almost stumbled over a handbag; rinsed her face, catching how red it was.

I can tell that was rudimentary French, the slightly bilingual Katrina thought, but it was still cute,

After looking it up and Google Translate and getting "he seems" at the end, she was very confused–but accepted that the site probably wrong.

Then she hopped into the shower, deciding to exfoliate her face there. The two lost sight, a long time ago, of what it meant to process and contain exactitudes. The telling to another person just what they meant to say and why. This led them down paths which tended to distort and sanitize their character, invalidating the truth. At different points, the pair of friends realized that proving a theory right or proving a rumor wrong on the Internet spaces was not cut for reality anymore.

Even though "none of you guys really know me" was a phrase that Maralyn often ran through her head, before and after deleting webpage shrines or crying over bad grades, she reached a point tonight just like many of the kids did or would: this doesn't work for me anymore.

And that was their omnipresent rationale. Ubiquitously.

The next day at school.

Her eyes are open wide. After zooming in on them, the camera glides to the students–pencils in their hands. Thick and lean, pale and light brown fingers can be seen holding them, recording responses on the test's last page. Then, it turns to black or otherwise dark, muscular and fat hands gripping onto their yellow sticks as if their livelihoods depend on their marks. And most of these are still on the first or second page of the exam, circling as many answers as they can, filling in bubbles when they conjure enough bravery to send their answers off.

Ms. Hortz stalks around the second group mostly. In circles, with a hurried look. Which the camera observes better than anyone else.

"Ah," the voice rings out, almost cracking.

The frame becomes blocked by the blonde teacher's torso, shaking around to show her thighs. We see Ms. Hortz rest a wary, trying-to-be-calm, and deliberate hand on Sage's shoulder.

The boy felt forceness in her touch–and too close and warm of a press from her clammy palm. He was too busy working to look up and somehow deal with it.

That usually meant staring down the aggressor until they hastily walked away. Him not doing so somehow made the sour taste in his mouth even more powerful. And it did not go away long after she picked up her hand four seconds later. She had probably lamely picking up that he was uncomfortable. As teachers were expected to recognize.

Throughout his next class, calculus, he wondered: Why did she do that to me?

Teachers were supposed to care too.

Walking by a girl with a Wendy's ice cream cone, the scary teacher reminded him of the ice part of the dessert. His intuition was clear, giving him these feelings. He bolted through the bleach and artificial smells in the main entrance hallway.

Linoleum tiles.

"Why do you keep on targeting her?" the watching boy asks, as if the characters were really there. "She didn't do anything." he wanted to say further, but kept inside. The institution's faults aren't her fault.

He huffs and turns the screen off.

Maybe I'll think about it later, he thinks.

No Moment

Picking at their acne. Telling them,
telling them–
Telling them: No. Not, no, not, don't–
no, it's wrong. Don't
You Can't Do It.
Giving space to (angelic) water.

"Tell them I said no." Ms. Genevieve something forcefully muttered to Mr. Ryedigger.

The deeply bigoted man's physicality was currently in line with his usual red and bloated cheeks.

"No. No, they cannot fucking do it," she repeated.

"You're right," he admitted, with a sigh. "No," he gently imitated, "Never in a million years."

Genevieve recoiled inside when she heard the moist sound his mouth made upon closing. Nevertheless, she was filled with admiration for the aging man and complete joy at their skills in persuading direction.

Power.

Irritation.

-

Maralyn grit her teeth (Josiah pulled through, goddamn it you know he pulled through); Henry made it through (and far) and the girls were fine; and you know Katrina and Trevor made it out Alright.

Scr-ibb,
les–Scratches; Scribbles–Scra–
.thces.

Intercept–Interruption–broken–broken down=breaking;

Finally/finally breaking down. Duh duh duh. Broken down.

"I wish you could be honest
With me"
–The Neighbourhood - "Honest"

She would follow her special girl anywhere, including Hell. She'd give up her volunteer idea, the video, it all, for her strange sake.

If the need ever arose to, she figured.

She saw that Katrina had Tweeted, °god i need some milk°

The study concluded that rather than being the product of willful discrimination, the bias was probably an outgrowth of subconscious cultural influences.
–Dan Bilefsky - "Women Respond to Nobel Laureate's 'Trouble With Girls'"

Chapter 7

At an indoor clearing, in between the cafeteria and the main elevators, the spot convened. They had been chillaxing there for half an hour, and the pizza order arrived 15 minutes ago. It was a very calm area of the B floor. Only B and C level kids really knew it existed, as it wasn't boujee enough for Sigma students and levels D and E contained only little kids. People could unofficially reserve it to cry or have lunch in groups, which is what was now happening.

Jesse strolled in rhythmically, with her Beats headphones in. They streamed a song by electronic and trap artist barnacle boi. Her moving stature seemed long and confident, and she only offered peripheral glances to the boys with glows upon their faces.

The eternally calm Heather followed afterwards, who had on new high-top Chuck Taylors. They were black, but she had painted them olive green while she was high the other night. She carried a stacked plate of only the cafeteria's best.

There were Styrofoam™ plates lining the curve of the ledge there. Josiah, Maralyn, and Christina were there already.

"You heard the new Lana Del Rey?" Jay asked Christina hurriedly, she was a fellow big fan of hers. All of the girls loved her music, though.

Maralyn seemed to be in a fixed gaze at something unreal, or not present in time currently. Her eyes shuddered around, in correlation with likeness to what they searched for. Seeing someone who looked like her; up and down and left and then quickly to the ground. Repeat. Catching someone who had had a crush on her, even years ago, anxious left and right, up and down and up. Hesitation.

She walked in, her feet silent almost, simply trying to concentrate on the music in her Apple earbuds. She was thinking of Fox (Foxen), a boy whom she was *talking* to. Her thick eyebrows, which sheltered bright eyes, penetrated Maralyn's vision.

"Well, hello there, you," Rosie said to Katrina, deviously beaming.

Shit, Maralyn thought–still incapacitated by her dizzy emotions.

"Hiii," Katrina responded. "What's going on?"

"Not much! We're just trying to find Rosie a boyfriend." Josiah answered shyly. "Can you help us, boo?"

"Oh sure." she quickly said. "Just make sure he's at least 5'8","

Every involved person burst out laughing.

"Oh my god," Christina said.

But before Katrina could add to that, she felt suddenly overwhelmed by an anxiety odd and paralyzing. It made her angry, actually pushing her to speak even more.

"And make sure you don't meet him on Tinder or something. Please. That shit is not worth it,"

"Oh my god." Christina replied. "Okay, well, I've met a couple cute guys on there. It's not as bad as people cut it out to be,"

"Yeah, like, so what?" Josiah added, largely ignored by the girls. "It's not like Grindr,"

"No, Christina? What the fuck are you talking about," Rosie said to her.

"Yeah seriously, that application is a vicious cancer. Most of the guys are weird or dumb as fuck, which I'm sure you know. And if you're bi, they just want you to join a threesome with their boyfriends. You're just not going to find a boy on there,"

"I think she's right," Jesse muttered.

"Alright, whatever you say," Rosie answered. "What do I do?"

"Meet people, talk to cute dudes at concerts or tea places or sports games or whatever. I don't know; you feel me,?"

Rosie affirmed her understanding, caressing Josiah's hand half-jokingly.

"I just want a cigarette," Jesse said.

"Same. I feel that." Maralyn abruptly, anxiously replied.

"I just want to listen to City and Colour," Katrina added.

What the fuck, Katrina–Maralyn thought.

She's Reaching, Your Honor

On the next night: Maralyn's group gathered. She couldn't make it because of family obligations, but hoped to join them next time. Twilight converged into darkness, with ice cold rain around them a fleeting yet stable image. They were a beautiful group of young kids, each carrying their own ways in fashion, telling stories in the way that they walked too.

Rosie's wavy brunette bob had in it a red streak after last weekend, but this was quickly fading away. She often complained about her hair, it being probably her number one insecurity. Her style was old, baggy shirts held in by tightly fitting high-waisted pants, the latter usually washed up or worn down. She usually wore bright colors, which went well with her fair white skin and moisturized red lips. Today, she wore Adidas Superstars that were formerly her brother's, with dry mud on them; he had barely touched them when they fit him. She was the one who organized this gathering.

°the square at 8, i just finished tennis° she had texted to the group conversation about an hour before.

The town was quiet, except for a noisy car driving past every now and then, plus the wind. There would be laughing, intoxicated couples rushing out of restaurants during the weekend, but this was a school night. The spots that they stood near were mostly closing. Three of them stood impatiently by Brett's small and old white Audi. It was slightly dirty on the outside, but the interior was dressed in speckless leather and Yankee candle.

Heather, with her long and straight dirty blonde hair, got dropped off down the street; nobody really noticed.

"Rosieee," she said blandly yet joyfully, while approaching her friends. She smirked at the others while going in to hug only Rosie. "I have arrived!"

"Alright, whore," Jesse said, side eyeing Heather as she walked away.

Rosie's jaw dropped while in the shape of a smile. She giggled.

"Come here too, you douchebag," Heather said, and they hugged tightly.

Jesse and Heather were into the same aesthetics, so they dressed nearly identically at times. They owned Tumblrs of black and white photos, plus posts about indie band updates and fan edits of members smoking cigarettes alongside their sad lyrics. There were contrasts with pictures of trees and waterfalls, and self-care advice. Each had their own demeanor and habits, but their clothing choices agreed: tall black Doc Martens with tight jeans, on their faces poignant lipstick in reds.

Heather wore a black leather jacket. Jesse sported a ripped up band t-shirt; her nose ring shined in the waning sun.

Brett asked, "What do you guys want to do?"

The group became silent. Each quietly respected his voice, common with him, although they did not immediately reply.

"I don't know," Jesse ended up muttering. She never knew what to do, so these words flew right up into the air, they were placeholders. "I'm not sure."

"Okay." he responded in his deep voice. "Let's just go to my house,"

The three girls nodded together.

12 minutes of smoking Marlboros in the car later, they tried to conceal their excitement in front of Brett. His house was always a good time, regardless of day or guests. He himself always made sure that things worked out. Otherwise, deep and strange anxieties ensued inside. Tonight, he wore a black Pyrex sweatshirt and sagging light blue jeans, with navy and orange Air Jordans. His dark brown hair ruffled upwards, showing sturdy masculinity alongside his physique.

"Alright," he mumbled, looking at the grass, occupied with a thousand ideas at once. He developed some aura of importance about him, which the girls focused on.

"What's up?" Rosie asked him.

"Get inside, yo,"

Soon, though, they'd go back to their rambling and forget about everything.

Rosie played music too loud for conversations to prolong, but her taste compensated for that. Her SoundCloud Reposts navigated through Brett's AUX cord and then speakers. The first song was "Faded" by Zhu.

It's very him, Rosie thought. Actually, it's very Dakota…

Heather chuckled to herself at the music. She yearned for The 1975 and The Doors, but accepted the dark electronic track.

It began to rain. The bedroom's windows quickly fogged up.

"Fuck!" Brett shouted after he heard the series' of thunder first clap.

"What's wrong?" Jesse asked him with concern in her voice.

"Did you want to smoke?" Heather asked calmly.

A song from Travis Scott's Owl Pharaoh mixtape, "Bad Mood/Shit On You," came into his mind, but he was too occupied with his friend's questions to find his phone to play it. The weather was worrying. He slapped his cheek in frustration. He opened his eyes widely, staring out blankly.

"Uhm," he responded. "Yeah, I did, but it's okay,"

"Oh," Jesse said, glaring back. "Yeah, it's okay. We can find something else to do; I don't know,"

We get it Jesse, thought Heather, you don't smoke weed. Jesus.

But her annoyance soon faded.

Rosie wanted very badly for this moment to be over.

"Okay come on, Brett. Just play your stuff and we can just enjoy the rain. We can smoke later if it stops, or go somewhere else," Rosie said.

"Enjoy?" Jesse asked sharply.

"Yeah?" she answered. "I don't know."

Brett plugged in his phone, turning up a miscellaneous Slum Village instrumental, then asked what the group wanted to listen to.

"It doesn't matter," Heather said quickly. "We're here,"

And the door was knocked.

Rosie asked, half-jokingly, "What's that? Who's creeping in?"

Brett made a bitter face at her while heading there animatedly.

The scent of cigarettes and fresh marijuana was like a gust to the girl at the door. She outstretched her hand to Brett. He held it for a moment, then she rested it on his sweatshirt pocket.

"Where's the weed," she quietly inquired. It was obviously not serious, but told him of her intentions. And he loved her for it.

"Huh, Brett?" Roberta, or Robbie to family, asked. "You gonna let me know?"

He laughed and she pushed her way in, following the scent to his room.

"What's up, ladies," she sassily asked in her raspy voice. "Everybody good? Where's Katrina? Josiah, Maralyn?"

"I don't know," Rosie replied. "They couldn't be here,"

"Wow, it sounds like they died. Rest in peace." she answered.

Ignoring Rosie and Heather laughing hard, Jesse reached for the crackers besides Brett's bed. The kid himself was rummaging through a cabinet in another room, they didn't know what for.

"Fuck this wack shit, we're playing the new Young Thug," Roberta announced–switching in her phone at the AUX.

The boy rushed back in happily after hearing the song, reaching in to hug Roberta. She accepted it and they smiled with their eyes at one another.

"Okay. May I ask why you guys are eating my food? Like, where did you even find those?"

They looked up at him with childlike, buggy eyes. Heather shrugged.

°hey man°

Brett wiped his eyes, then abandoned the group again for a moment to reply to Josiah's text. Meanwhile, they attempted to turn on Netflix using Brett's PlayStation.

°Waddup°

°chilling°

Josiah added soon after, °wondering if you want to bake out°

Brett made a quizzical face with tight lips. He thought, who says that?

°Yea let's do it° he replied.

°okay, i'll be over now !°

Brett quickly responded, °Wait no, i have people over°

°well what should i do thenn°

°One sec°

The dizzy boy put his phone in his pocket and heard Jesse in his hallway. He approached her because she was the first person he saw next.

"Yo," he said, grabbing onto her arm.

She looked confusedly at him.

"Yeah?"

"Where is everybody?" he asked, hesitant.

"In your room…"

"Okay," he replied, embarrassed for a moment.

Then he went back to his average sized bedroom. Jesse followed. The floor in the hall was freshly cleaned, so the wood was a glossy, dark brown. The walls were an off white. After he approached his door on the left with speed, he turned the knob and left it open for Jesse.

"Hey, Brett!" someone yelled. He didn't know who or why but ignored it.

"Guys," he spoke.

Rosie had her head in Heather's lap in his room. Every girl reclined crunched on Brett's full-sized bed. They looked up at him inquisitively, hoping with all of them against bad news.

"Josiah wants to come over,"

Rosie's eyes lit up.

"Um, okay?" Heather replied.

After a long pause, he asked, "Do we do it?"

"Boooo," Jesse calmly stated, referring to Josiah, or at least Josiah coming over.

Everybody silently looked around, thinking about the concept and trying not to burst out in laughter.

Rosie caved in first, "Does he want to smoke with us or something?"

"It's raining," Jesse said.

"Yeah I fuckin' know." the girl replied. "But we can just go under something or use umbrellas. And why don't you guys want him here?"

"You have umbrellas, right?" Heather asked.

"Uh yeah, I think so," His words blurred into each other. His mumbles were quiet yet/but still pronounced.

Like that, the topic of Josiah joining them was set aside.

They did their usual things, like watching Nickelodeon reruns, smoking kush, and laughing at one another. Heather and Jesse had rummaged Brett's parents' closet, with his permission, for an umbrella–they found three. During the sunset, Heather reminisced on Trevor and Maralyn's song demos, with a smile in her eyes. Comfortable and safe on Brett's porch, she wondered if the music was available anywhere online.

In the future, that night would seem to have gone by very quickly.

There's No Such Thing as New Wave

God is a punk song, and the drums are great.

It won't be said that the drummer is great because some people, like Donovan Melero or Paul McCartney, are multitalented. Benzos are really fucked up, but they inspire good music. "I hate when my idols die," a young kid (fails to) realize.

Just stretch. Roam. Be free.

Somebody died for you–and they have multiple and many manifestations. Whatever pronouns. That's God, that's nirvana.

Oh, man. The way people look at each other when they're in the driver's seat. Ridiculous. Obnoxious. Especially where Sigmund, Sigma, Siegfried–what was it?, kids hail from.

Gotta love 'em, though.

Gotta appreciate any teenage kid for what they are. Anyways, crabby middle-aged men and women, in specific. It's like they have nothing better to do than reflect on their pisspoor adolescent romantic decisions that got them into these buttcrack jobs anyways, and project onto the kids and try to fix things. It was your fault for ignoring fate, for turning down God's shy calls. Don't make yourself the victim. These people need to be there for their kids,

That was something Maralyn and her mother often discussed, in hushed but compassionate tones–in the kitchen or drive from school.

"You know what's wrong now,
You can't deny this"
–The Last Drag - The Samples

The cigarette's white made her eyes tear up. It was a shocking burning sensation, getting the smoke in her eyes for the first time.

"Oh fuck,"

She was embarrassed. Didn't particularly care though, it hurt. It looked like she was crying now.

"Yeah," Trevor hesitated. "You'll be okay,"

Katrina texted him. He brought the phone to his face to read it. The boy grunted.

Shut the fuck up…he thought. Go smoke your cigarette, and then think about God a little. For christ's sake,

Meanwhile, Maralyn was hacking away.

"Bro, do you need some water?" he asked.

"Nah, nah, dude. I'm good,"

"Alrightie,"

And with that, the two finished their Newport 100s in peace.

"Ha," she said, after a pause, her voice weakening. "Remember when we made that song,"

He inhaled deeply, looking away as if to change the subject.

"Anyways," she replied.

"Right,"

"I warned the proud, 'Stop your boasting!' I told the wicked, 'Don't raise your fists! Don't raise your fists in defiance at the heavens or speak with such arrogance.'"

Dawg.

For no one on earth--from east to west, or even from the wilderness--should raise a defiant fist. It is God alone who judges; he decides who will rise and who will fall.

At home now. Maralyn reclined with her feet on the granite counter. She had been spent a lot of the day like that, with her wine glass of iced coffee, scanning Reddit.

Her parents left the rest of the house as is when they purchased it, but they were adamant on upkeeping the basement. In front of Maralyn was a nine foot wide wooden cabinet filled with alcohol and exotic glasses. Standing in front of it, it became a mirror, nearly perfect due to her dad cleaning it every Sunday. But this evening, she did not feel pressure to spin or poke at her face there.

Josiah picked up Maralyn, the next morning, and they headed to the mall.

Her clammy palms and black denim jacket smelled heavily of rosemary and eucalyptus oils. Maralyn sprayed her outfit with these aromas before leaving, and used a diffuser for a room the day before.

The steel chairs and table here felt cold on their hands and butts, so the two stood up to wait for their smoothies instead. There was a small group of other quiet waiters. Each individual or pair were far enough not to hear the others' conversations. Plus, all the machines blasted on high. They were here for smoothies with too much sugar.

"Ivy" by Frank Ocean played overhead.

Jay turned to Maralyn fairly quickly and said, "So, What's up?"

At first, she only quizzically glared at him. He then knew that there was maybe something confusing or hurting her. He hoped that it was just bothering her–widening his eyes and starting to smile.

"We're not getting anywhere with the meetings and protesting." Maralyn said with a down, coarse tone. "I know we have to wait until we see results happen, but I feel like I can't wait that long,"

Throughout this, Josiah nodded or shook his head, at the right intervals. In affirmation, like a charismatic interlocutor. He had the intuition of a good friend. His wits were sharp for his loved ones.

"You're just too hurt at this point," he said plainly.

"Yes. Exactly. I think I should hold on and keep meeting with the group, but with my own reservations. It's good for experience, too,"

Jay said, purely emotionally, definitely striking a deep cord in the air around them, "They just don't give a fuck about us,"

Maralyn nodded. She had a sour feeling her stomach. She thought about taking a Tums out of her bag, but remembered what a few Sigma kids had said a few years ago. "Those are so trashy," with laughs.

Josiah was in discomfort, as well. If his heart was a cozy pile of orange leaves, it flew around everywhere now. It had been doing so. He swallowed these feelings in understanding and sympathy.

"I. I just wish I didn't remember it," Maralyn said, about the meeting. "I wish I wouldn't remember it,"

He nodded.

They sipped on their smoothies and transitioned into leaving.

Josiah's random SoundCloud likes played through his old but good speakers. On their drive home.

And, "Peace out," she told her friend, closing the door. He replied with a cool peace sign, and then they split ways.

Maralyn was surprised for a second to find the front door unlocked, but she simply headed straight to her bed. Standing up had been making her extremely nauseous.

There was a dreary cold seeping into her room from all the cracks and openings. She did not do her bedtime routine–which often just transpired as a show, for nobody there. Fantasies did not envelop her mind that night. The white and deep blue bed set was arranged sloppily from early that morning. Her hair was a display of frays and dead ends, her lone halo of tangibility. Maralyn flopped onto the mattress. A long but short moment went by, including a steep stare into oblivion; she fell asleep.

In her dreams, she Tweeted:

°some people don't feel real, or aren't made to be real in our world°

°so isn't it fit, and kind of just almost, that they would pray to something not material?°

°why is that a social crime… how are you going to tell them their worship is wrong when their whole lives have been in the clouds?°

Chapter 8

Running Through The 666 With My Woes

Monday. All of Opifer was cold and in Middleton, a freshman boy slipped on the recently mopped floors. Large students' shoes squeaked when they twisted or bounced around their friends. A few kids had brought dirt tracks in with them, drying pieces of brown crust flinging across the floor. There were some shredded grass leaves.

The group crept through the hallways. Katrina ate an apple for breakfast while clutching her cardigan, mainly holding it because it didn't match her outfit. Dakota led the way towards the lobby.

In the main office, they would sign up for the Pre-Project Dance. It asked for a five dollar fee which would help Middleton with concessions. The line was already long, lunch having ended only two minutes ago, so the boy in the front made it a point for them to hurry.

"Why are you guys only doing this now?" Christina, a senior, asked.

The tall blonde girl walked alongside Heather, who was paired with Sage. He seemed lonely, but he always composed humbly, so any darkness was hard for them to tell. Henry was behind them alongside Josiah, and Trevor lagged behind staring at his phone.

"Um, sorry, I forgot," Dakota responded.

"Yeah, but it's so late," she blurted back. "Like we've had since February to do it."

Oh my god, shut the fuck up, Christina, Josiah thought. He noticed Henry discreetly roll his eyes and copied him.

"It's not a big deal, girl," Dakota voiced softly.

"First of all, don't ever call me that. And second, you guys are so lazy! And you literally have until tomorrow to get it done," She had begun smiling, but her light eyes seemed to be watering with embarrassment.

"Good thing we're doing it right fucking now," Dakota sternly mumbled.

And with that, it was over. Relief. Henry was prepared to get to class. Although he hated pre-calculus, anything to get away from that girl slash acquaintance slash ex-potential-lover. Josiah felt kind of disappointed that everybody shut up; he ran from responsibility and any reminder of it. He already had a piano recital tomorrow night to prepare for, and a valley of dolls in his closet to upkeep. Doing well in school was because of his parents. Rosie felt pretty as they glided by the freshmen in the different hallways. She especially loved Henry's nervous faces in groups like this. Bonus points if he took the time, with deep green eyes, to impress random cute girls. Dakota's forward gaze was empty–in a comfortable way– to her. The group roamed about the school, indefinite in their gross spokesmanship of nihilism.

Swallow It and Move On

One could make a living inside of a distraction.

With her.

That was her, a living shoot into another plane of existence. Not a higher or lower one, but something right and good on the current level. She would often be calling and calling, "Join me," "Come inside, here," Those looks straight up into the sky, or eyes resting on the ceiling a long while. Inviting presence. A person, the pinnacle of distraction. Aesthetically pleasing.

The sun shone directly on Maralyn's forehead, gently spilling into her eyes. She was daydreaming.

She wondered about that one a lot. As a surprising, tingling presence throughout her body, she could see how the girl could hurt those close to her like she did. Empathy did its thing, gracefully. The thoughts were kind of chilling. Maralyn suddenly snapped out of the few moments daze and quickly got up to start doing more chores. Later, when she sat back down to take a break with orange juice and a Poptart, her mouth was bitter like her mind. But the sun did not neglect her tired back.

One Hell of A Distraction

Checking the screen is compulsory.

And so he does it.

The wise and elderly man with the long, mountainous beard: “In order to achieve the higher state, you must let go of all pretense which suggests that you are already there. Don’t listen to yourself; don’t listen to voices in your mind.”

After a pause, possibly unintentional from the developers, he states, “When you are there, you won’t feel, smell, touch, or hear it, you will know it. It will be your everything. You will have become life itself.”

The boy only puts his head down. The voice sees his buzzcut.

“Fear is a voice in your head. There will be no voices in your head.” The last words he spoke were, “Are you scared?”

The projected image begins to shake, as well as growing darker as if somebody is turning down the machine’s brightness.

Fear is exceedingly excited energy. Exciting.

The rectangles (almost square) windows inside the frame let in and out light.

Thank you for focusing on me.

On the lower hemisphere, the structure reveals a man walking from right to left, and a woman, who seemed black from behind. This makes us trusting of the environment–touched, almost blessed, by her comforting and brilliant strength. But when her face surfaces, it turns out that she is Asian. Filipino or Indonesian. Exotic. She has a great, brilliant smile on. We still feel trusting of the environment.

"I could breathe
in and out
But I probably won't"

is what Maralyn transcribes to a notebook.

Kurt: you were basically a martyr, she then realizes. What is a martyr?

So many female rappers could be viewed as the greatest, but all they do is fight, Katrina thought.

She thought about violence, physical, tonight. While reclining on the old couch in her living room, her parents' favorite to do paperwork or cuddle in, tattered in some places.

You know, I wish people knew, that it's so pointless. And it gets us nowhere. It's not worth it in the scheme of things, because we're just hurting people. We remember people by how they make us feel. That's what Maya Angelou said. We're just going to hold on to the pain, and the pain caused to us by attacking them, and only remember that. Only learn that, how they made us feel that way. There ain't no room for dialogues or learning something new, or being shown what we're supposed to see. Someone who physically harms someone is holding onto something, trying to prove something or tell them something.

That just doesn't work after you fight. The phrase "lol" then surfaced in her mind. She chuckled.

It was evening, but she there experienced mighty sunbeams peeking through their tall windows. Maybe it was her mind.

Chapter 9

The next morning. Before getting in the car with Elias. Searing. Dark, calm. Read this like 1, 2, 3. “A, B, C.” Hard workers knew how to work hard. But how did they learn it?

No thank you for so quickly forgetting about my voice and me. Psychopath. Nah, no storm clouds. Storm clouds in the mind. Cringeworthy. Please look that word up if you are stupid.

“You can’t put your heart against
because I don’t have a chest”

were the words that she wrote down now.

“How could I ever right my wrongs?
sweetie?
How could I change myself to be more like you?
Why do you only give me light?

Girl?”

Maralyn’s thoughts next were: you wanted me to write an essay that was logical, started with a thesis statement, and was perfectly ordered.

Sighed. Breathed.

Fuck all you. You know, I don’t want to hate on you. I don’t want to be hateful, right now. Or ever, really, I don’t think it’s good for me. I just want to breathe it in like smoke,

The siblings were driven to school.

-

A few hours after a meeting which the friends had signed up to "improve Opifer's social environment." The meeting had been turbulent, and utterly disturbing for most– some more than others.

They stayed in the school after getting the rest of they day off, sitting still, waiting for every person to have a ride before splitting off again.

"You know, Maralyn," Rosie warmly said, facing her and the others. "I'm really glad I got through to you today, and the whole presentation did really,"

Heather nodded in agreement.

"Yeah. It seems like that's been something you've been keeping in for a long time," she spoke in her deliberate fashion.

They were referring to the major sense of anxiety which sometimes fell over the girl, especially during school.

"All my life, I've felt like I have to prove somebody wrong, or fix a bad idea of me," she emotionally told the group. Deep inside, there was a concrete part of her that wanted to abide by this obligation which hurt her, yet she had to recognize the pain for what it could do to her. "It's a big... in a sense, it's a big feeling of being trapped. As corny as that sounds. And not really being able to talk to someone for help because your mind has confined you to a particular frame that you can't see outside of."

Before her last sentence, many audience members had stopped listening out of both hyperactive and somber sense of relatability. They couldn't all completely relate.

"So the help doesn't seem like it's there, like it exists at all," Her voice shook on the last part, but it was okay because everyone was clearly supporting her.

The squad filled each of a circular table's seven seats, two of the chairs holding backpacks. Josiah's blue Jansport bag was thick from the two textbooks inside and was open. Binders and notebooks were splayed out on the table. They were supposed to be doing homework and studying for tests together. A conversation began, and soon enough the arm of the Projects reached them. Or the eye. It caught them in an idle moment of scholarly enjoyability, and snatched away those rights.

Because that's what it did. Displeasure was inherent in its nature. Every kid dreaded doing the Projects.

Half green and half orange leaves fell with a soft landing as their undersides pushed against the air. The windows to their left or right showed what the environment outside was doing. There was slight condensation on the outer edges of the rectangular tiles, where tiny oval shaped leaves stuck to the glass.

"I think," Maralyn said with a heavy deliberation. "I want to do my Project video on..."

And that is where the blackout began. She heard Mr. Ryedigger's scratchy, scratching voice bouncing around her subconscious.

There were some imaginary yells, but the nausea was real. Physical shadows of the disorientation, the powerlessness, the speechlessness. Ego deleted, he was a terrible person.

I'm so sorry, she suddenly heard in her mind. It made her feel warm, safe, then she quickly brushed it off.

"–about the due date or something?"

"Yeah, everything is going to be okay…you guys," Rosie said calmly.

"You right," Josiah added.

The patient and softspoken Jesse asked all, "What are you all doing tonight?"

"Probably going to my mom's house, then making a fat bubble bath," from Rosie.

"Talking to Maralyn about this supposed video idea." Jay said, giving Maralyn a fake suspicious look.

I just want to listen to The Rolling Stones, she thought.

Rosie's mom had texted her that she was here, at their favorite lot. The rest parted ways to Jesse's SUV and Josiah to his car. Their webbed conversations about sensitive topics were all over. It was time to go home. They went home. They arrived at their homes.

M and J had ended up getting an A- on their research paper–but after much arguing after-school with Ryedigger and Genevieve, via Mr. Willis and Allen. Topics included if they could both handle the "social responsibility" of the ideas and design it "up to par" (per an email) with the Project standards. After that much talking about it, Maralyn didn't even feel as inspired about their thesis (which was that students of color felt proportionally less safe and comfortable in Opifer). It had lost her, the energetic influence escaped her. It all had been stolen.

Maralyn quickly saw that Rosie had Tweeted, °It's really important that your friends respect you and your dreams°

She simply smiled, didn't look at any of the responses. And whoever knew about their strange day would just have to learn about it. She locked her iPhone and tossed it onto the nightstand.

About to sleep, Maralyn had quietly on a playlist with some Title Fight songs–she manually queued only those. She turned over. Her lower body felt basically weightless, but the mind filled with a significant type of matter; her head felt heavy. It processed most of her present energy. Her heart was clear from attention to the outside world.

Later in the journey, her hand grabbed at a white and dark purple, wet orb, reminiscent of a fantastical egg–first passing through a white t-shirt. Then, she turned over and over and over. Arbitrary lines inside:

> "*What's the point in not listening?*
> *There isn't one*
> *Don't worry about things like that*
> *U dig*"

Then, the Projects.

Since Maralyn was a junior, she really wanted the actor to be mature-looking, to gain the respect of the audience (especially the adults and Trevor and Katrina). She envisioned a bony yet toned 5'9" white boy with long blonde hair, headbanging to their alternative rap song–Josiah's muffled vocals trickling in and the artificial guitar growling. There it was, she realized, the grandeur and brilliance of their youth; going somewhere finally (that nobody else is supposed to know); all of her friends nearby.

She decided then that she would cut away relaxation and hanging out time to work to manifest these visions. Although it wasn't natural, she imbued certainty to the idea that Josiah would be completely supportive. The fact that he would. She was his partner, after all. She would make this happen.

This music is so ass, she thought–when a folk or country or whatever type song came on shuffle. I need to sleep,

Okay. Finally. Goodnight,

A harsh resistant sound of a chair against carpet went by. It broke the silence of shame, similar to a cricket or breeze.

"Well, okay," Mr. Willis said loudly, practically shivering. "Mr. Ryedigger,"

"What shall we do, 'shall our kids do, next, if their society is so corrupted?" "We're gathered here today for an open and intellectual discussion about our students' comfort at Opifer. You know, regarding the make-ups and such. And, quite honestly, I am just starting to feel as if some of our students here are *confused* or not really, *completely,* understanding your point of view."

The overweight, round man took everybody's wait as a chance to belch fully, keeping it in his mouth and swallowing, even holding his stomach afterwards. He let the pleasure seep in for a few moments, then signaled that he was thinking of what to reply.

Good fucking lord, Maralyn thought.

Many students shifted around or looked away, perturbed.

"We need to resort back into the status quo," the friends heard him say. "And trust our *strong*, tough men and young boys to do the dirty work. Do you know what I mean? Do I make sense now?"

Mr. Willis, plus several of Maralyn's friends, had muddled eyebrows.

Oh good lord. We're not going to reason with this guy, Josiah thought.

Maralyn decided to take the initiative and vocalize a problem behind the meeting called. Or two.

"Mr. Ryedigger," and when her teachers shot her looks, "Mr. Willis, if I may–there are several homophobic and racist problems plaguing Opifer. Specifically, at Middleton last year, a student who is African American that I know was called the n-word by a fellow peer. They were sitting in class and it supposedly happened in a discussion about their cultures or something, their cultural differences."

Although Mr. Willis and all of her friends' face were red now, she continued, "And the other day at Sigma, a boy student who identifies as gay was shoved around in the hallway–the bullies are always bullying him for his sexual orientation. What do you say to that? What should we do about that?"

Genevieve gulped, knotting her sweaty hands together. The teachers present contributed a silence that spoke: well, there you go. And?

The students rose their voices in support of these issues. They went back and forth with a man who dodged and redirected questions, continually citing the school's academic excellence. Maralyn simply stared down at her lap, making sure to sit up straight.

Exiting the room once the meeting was finally over, a few students quietly patted her on the back.

"That's what humans do, and we fail,
Sometimes air is just okay,
Okay, goodnight."

Chapter 10

Other people keep us from going insane. Other humans keep us from falling into lonesome, isolated Narcissus fate. Keep us from denoting ourselves prophets– superiority-complexed individuals driven by an insane mission and vision to save the really already good world by exterminating all the bad. Keep us from lying lonely at night, punching ourselves over guilt and mistakes, and not understanding how to live life when it is light. Keep us from feeding ourselves poisons (nicotine, alcohol, drugs.) in order to feel emotions or run away from emotions.

The root cause of insanity is biology and loneliness.

Maybe. Maybe one day. Maybe one day Maralyn will smile, or know how to.

Inputting commands nonstop, she thinks about Dakota and Sage's cologne and deodorant, then figures safety out of the memory of Katrina's large hands.

Let us continue. Move on.

Have some hope.

"You could never set me free,
Buddy
Baby"
–Trevor - "The Sun Never Sets on Teenagers" (a demo for a possible Project song)

Even Though They May Drive Us Insane

The red balloon that they had tied around a chair arm flew up high now. Josiah's short and chunky dad boomed to him and his cousins, "Where is Uncle Sheng!?"

"Dad, oh my god!" his son botheredly replied.

His father simply smiled, red cheeks smushed like a cute tomato, and waved.

"Hey!" he exclaimed even louder.

Josiah asked Maralyn cynically, "Can you tell that he smokes,"

She sighed in slight shock. "Josiahh, it's okay,"

He rolled his eyes.

"Fuck that shit," he muttered.

The kids, like Josiah's favorite little cousin Brian, made a ruckus in the air with their field games and leaking bubble blowers. They made remnants everywhere with their chocolately fingers, having rummaged the ancient depths of Josiah's pantry for snacks.

Maralyn had to leave early to have dinner with her extended family at home. The cousins on both sides were coming over in 45 minutes to feast on quzi and dolma. When it was time to escort her, while his family was deep into the barbeque, the entire yard invaded by smoke, Josiah stood nearby like a lone young wolf.

She was saying her goodbyes to his family–"Thank you for having me, the food was really good!"–and he almost couldn't let go of the concept of the porch door. The rectangle structure loomed over him. He slowly derealized, images of his father and him arguing at the piano years ago forming and disintegrating. Crumbling.

"Hello? Josiah," Maralyn spoke to her unresponsive friend. She chuckled nervously, "I have to go. Thank you for having me, bye,"

"Oh," he responded in a hushed, breathy tone. "Okay. Bye,"

All the Pain In Our Bodies

The next day.

At Maralyn's house.

The girl, with her light brown eyes which often seemed to glow, lay on her back on the floor. She ended up in that position after exerting much effort to scrub away Taco Bell cheese sauce from the rug. It had landed on a white portion.

Tonight, she thunk. And shut and opened her eyes tightly, twisting her fists against her temples. The girl reflected on chemicals that caused addiction. Dopamine, serotonin, adrenaline, something like that–she read it in a psychology magazine.

Beyond that, she quickly landed beyond that, she needed it again. The special fix of a substance or a certain lover was a mean vacuum beyond comparison, but she could always remind herself that it was her doing the inspiring. Simple, no staleness, never expiring; she would scratch her scalp until it scabbed and always hurt herself (nobody else); no blaming.

Where then, she did not wonder now, did the consequence end up? Probably in unforeseen places, at unpredictable times. in society, including the sources, like the store and the parents of the lovers. Naïve people like her assumed that all bad consequence would end up in their own lives and bodies. Yet, yet, yet. Other people breathed in their smoke, too.

Her eyes were shut, the thoughts too complex to completely understand right now. And then a new realization dawned upon her, this one lighter. Better.

The way the people around us feel is the way we feel. So, maybe being alone is good, other people's confidence, or lack of it, won't rub off on me. I'll get to be myself. I'll get to be on my own and stuff.

After standing up a few minutes later, her vision blacking out, the girl stared at the tall narrow mirror in the corner.

And thought that she was beautiful.

The moment also gave her insight as to how other people saw her. This revelation gratified her, like a hot coffee soon after waking up on Monday. Her eyes brightened like with their own minds, waking up the rest of her body. With all parts of her awake now, Maralyn went into the bathroom to wash her face and brush her teeth. The sink water was very cold but she did not notice it. She moisturized her skin, beginning with the plump cheekbones, then applied a thumb of jojoba oil mixed with rosemary oil to her neck.

She then slid into bed and fell sleep. It was a miracle that she immediately fell asleep with that much energy. So much of it was paradoxical, too. Or maybe that was how it was supposed to be. Sleeping well because of contentment; because of being human.

Almost Semester 2

Good morning.

"Wake up."

Everything changed when winter came around.

"Everything fucking changed when winter came around," Sage said to himself, at his house in his room.

The way somebody's closed eyes create upturned semi-circles, perfectly dark, no matter how their skin is pigmented. The young girl found solace in that image as she wrote down–bled out, cut herself and bled out, more–some thoughts and feelings.

A great weight was upon Maralyn, always entering from the side and resting on top of her head and then back. There is no use in writing fast, drawing fast…studying fast, she thought. There's no use in doing things like that.

People in her world wanted to make brain implants that would, besides introducing potentially hazards to the fragile organ, allow instant communication, browsing, and recording. These real ideas were not out of a Don DeLillo or Isaac Asimov book, they were real ideas. Maralyn, with her base understanding of biology, understood that every revolutionary invention (from these years forth, in the post-Steve Jobs generations) should be guided into fruition with checks and balances. A high sense of them. Yeah, that would help us, so she thought and sort of wrote down.

She convulsively put her notebook away. I'm still in motherfucking high school, she thought.

My existence is that extra tertiary layer added–she thought while staring at the bathroom mirror–whatever that means.

"No more being scared, Katrina."

His voice powers through the multiple glitches in the screen, due to the series of circular cracks in the left. It is a recording, but she doesn't know.

"You be you and do what you must."

It weighs in on her. It weighs in on her every second still.

"Okay? Alright, fine," she responded.

These kids, they were damaged by the screens. Weren't they? The screens did nothing to them, but they still screamed at them.

It was only possible to generalize and label from a complete stranger's point of view: "people who do drugs have easy, serene lives," "children who 'party' a lot have horrible or neglectful parents," "teenagers with gay inclinations are messed up in the head" and beyond.

Chapter 11

I don't know how to tell you how badly our misunderstandings hurt me, she wanted to say to her.

She was looking right at her, but nobody was there and nobody looked or heard.

This is a hard, difficult relationship…and friendship,

Katrina's "speech" voice was delicacies to Maralyn's ears. M unconsciously provoked political and social arguments out of her–so that she could be in the direct line of fire of her emotions and elements.

"You see, like, we can't even process what happens to use because we are constantly judging each other, and then we have the older generations talking down on us,"

We're constantly surrounded by each other, Maralyn thought.

Did not say because she felt like she would oddly wink if she did so; forever feeling awesome admiration in any of their agreements. Their conversation was not human.

"Yeah," Maralyn pushed her on. "And spreading lies. Or mistruths," she corrected herself.

Her takes weren't hot or heated, in her opinion, they were warm. She looked up at K's hair, to which that one swiped her hand over it and dramatically looked away. Maralyn pushed her on.

"Do you think that, like, ….." she asked, with slip-ups and hesitations.

Katrina hadn't even fully responded to her, the rest of the conversation negligible.

They then reached cigarette brands and Trevor's interesting family story (inciting just a little bit of jealousy from Maralyn), and their moment was done.

The weekend would come along. And pass.

The World (And Its Eyes)

I don't need to figure out what she's thinking, Trevor reflected while whipping open Instagram. This'll do it for me,

A bright and active page was what he glared at for a couple minutes.

Notifications came in and ever-awake "stories" were updated. The boy tended to not sense time during these invasive excursions. Now, this was probably because of guilt, about his private escapes from the moral responsibilities of the civilized world. But it just felt like escaping, plus getting to know people better, even. Which still made time feel less real, and the truth more concrete. He was simply "stalking."

Next her profile. It was the second suggestion after a profile titled °Smoky Ridge: Tobacco and Vape Shop Official IG°.

He understood his anxiety as it shook through his hands and vision.

Become alone, rapidly open a social media app, search for the name, and scan. Emotional nihilism built after each step of this. But then he would be done–when his eyes ached from the meaningless brightness. His identifiable anxiety would be intermittent during; and no brushing it away, no processing it. Neutral, digital, one or one hundred.

"Ain't No Sunshine When She's Gone," the child Michael Jackson version, blasted from his laptop. He had upgraded from Spotify to Apple Music recently, but had to update the program on his computer. The program lagged on his old PC. Trevor grunted whenever he got up to change the song.

A vision of the kids Trevor worked with every Tuesday and Thursday appeared in his mind after he noticed no new updates in Katrina's profile.

It was a blaring image; they ran around the community center's courtyard, seeming to all shout out their gibberish at once. But he could discern their unique voices, still, twenty-nine in total.

The after-school club for disadvantaged inner-city youths sparkled with success in its first year. It was his good friend Elisa's idea to start it. She oversaw meetings for two years now with a local social worker and her favorite teacher, from Sigma, Mrs. Romy. The latter was second generation Lebanese woman of a strong demeanor and build. Elisa was random seeming to his regular friends, like the group and such, which he was conscious of but did not care. The girl was very kind and that was all that he could have wanted. Should have wanted, as he often reminded himself. Trevor reflected with joy on the first meeting of the year, occurring back in October. The group gathered at a vast and entirely foggy park downtown. The nice part of the city; inside their bounds of safety.

Elisa often questioned the legitimacy of those concerns, though. Not because she believed that there were *no* safe areas, like many from her area did, but because there were so many other beautiful and worthwhile parts of the city. And so close by. Why did they have to serve within futile, intangible bounds? As long as you aren't alone and childlike, Elisa felt, who you are is irrelevant when it comes to experiencing this great place.

Still, outside of the bounds, the city contained dangerous potential. But, the founder of the service organization (Elisa disliked the word "charity") strolled with as much pride and trust as she would in her own neighborhood or a Sigma hallway.

Trevor was submerged in thought. He did not put his phone down, he could not; he kept scrolling through social media. One app and post after the other, over and over.

He saw in his mind the watery remains of a squashed up red popsicle. It formed a pond of translucent juice, almost resembling blood. It was a little image, the object lying on the play area's crackled black top. Its seep into the crevices gave only the illusion of coagulation. Boys had been playing basketball. Several of them black, one Latino, two white. They yelled orders with sportsmanship, huffing as they passed the energy along the court. They slammed teases at each other–with that same effective spirit. Trevor supervised it all, but really just stood in admiration.

Now. The social content was getting boring. All done. Close the suitcase and store it away. Trevor's thoughts about that far afternoon began to trail off. He didn't even realize that he locked his phone, sighed, and firmly set it on his nightstand. He got up to take a shower.

°Thanks for coming 2day !!° Elisa texted to Trevor, dated 7:52 pm.

He immediately opened it.

She was cute.

"So, in this course you will be completing various studies for the video portion of your Project." the neither thick nor thin, but chubby, white woman said.

Mrs. Millington said that in a tired, yet still compact and direct way. Her dry grey hair was well taken care of, contrasting with eyes that inevitably told of old age. Photos of her former self, with a classic silky blonde hairstyle and joined by some kind of sailor man, were in frames around the room.

"As many of you already know, I'm not all that familiar with technology." she said more quietly. "But you will be graded and judged by how well you get accustomed to it in here and utilize it in creative ways."

A few groans sounded throughout the room. This was the beginning of the end.

Maralyn and Jay were seated at opposite ends; constantly looking up at one another whenever she said something funny or horrible.

The teacher rotated her head–not breaking her confident, grounded pose in one single way. Her scan of the room was menacingly slow. Aliyah, nearly reclining in her seat at the very front, could clearly discern the frozen sky blue details of those eyes. They tinged on green, but it was totally unattractive, not a good mixture. The teacher sent rushed and angered cues to every one of the students, without forming a moment of eye contact with any of them.

To the athletic boy next to Aliyah, only wearing Under Armor and Nike, her gaze seemed like a red laser beam, penetrating every pupil. Ready to fire. Firing.

Maralyn had spent moments locking on Mrs. Millington's face, even after being denied the usual satisfaction of a look back. Mrs. Millington had in her something receding, as well as foggy with the anxiety normally adorning teenagers. Perhaps she had absorbed it. And a boy also in the front thought that she harnessed the Lochness monster or another one inside of her.

Maralyn simply stared on. Rebellion began to brew inside, about this class and that person, while she tried to take notes. Millington was going on about requirements and deadlines, onlooked by a nervously hopeful Mr. Allen. Whether she wanted to be rebellious or not did not satisfy her base question: why would a teacher introduce herself in such a distant, accusatorial way? Why would she be so like that, in the first place?

And she looked at Jay, as if to say: "Did you see that glare at me? That was a subtle little move. She seems to have a lot of subtle moves, but I caught that one. Do you see this?"

Her face was blanked out in sternness and slight disgust.

Jay silently responded, even nervously chuckling out loud, "We're going to skip this class a lot,"

Maralyn nodded.

They both would have preferred to switch out to another teacher completely, but all Project-related classes were required. And counselors did not accept small reasons for changing teachers, plus the classes were always full, so that was out of the question.

The brightness of the day through the windows was more emphasized now, especially after Millington finally let go–speaking to Mr. Willis who came in with a question. Voices rose and phones were checked. But then the man with unusually large eyes left the room. Nearly evacuated. He sympathetically glanced at Maralyn's friends and Mr. Allen while heading out.

The atmosphere reverted to "back to business; no questions." When she saw that the bickering was silencing and frightened faces calmed down (after looking at her again), Mrs. Millson resumed at once.

"You all already know that you can succeed in your Project with a multitude of creative options, it is not limited to producing videos. There are poster design, presentation, educational, and other options available. 93% of Opifer students prefer the videos, but we emphasize the student's own freedom and skill." It sounded as if she was reading from off of a transcript. "As long as it is organized and sensible, we will accept it and even support it."

In really real reality, the Creative portions made the students so unified because they, unofficially, provided a respite from schoolwork and the Volunteering research papers. The school manual, though, stated that they "may offer more opportunity for our artistically proficient students." They offered more opportunity for every student, because most of the kids enjoyed participating in them and so shone their talents and knowledge more.

"Directors" such as Mrs. Millington and Mr. Allen were tasked with spotting students who could not only meet, but surpass, expectations–and still be well-rounded. Who also enjoyed this and found it easy. For example: if an 11th grader could balance chemical equations, play varsity soccer, have friends, and write uniquely, they were more than good in the book. Such students gained the benefits of the adults' respect and an increased likelihood of A or A- Creative grades.

"Alright, folks,"

The signpost awoke several students–because finally something new, any transition was good.

"As promised, we will be doing a few little icebreakers, to hopefully get to know one another or form bonds, and so I can learn your names."

Rocks dropped into the stomachs of the socially anxious; every student signaled frustration. But it was better than hearing Millington's voice, especially droning on. The first activity she announced was perhaps the most simple icebreaker in existence: share your name, favorite animal, and one goal you have for this course.

The savage cold of the troposphere frosted their necks and the fragile earth. Lives could end swiftly like the Titanic now, but their breathing persisted. Maralyn stepped forward one more time, and the regular space-time continuum decayed as she began her descent into the cool, raw blackness.

The ice was breaking. Everybody and the huskies by their sides glared her way. There was complete silence until Mrs. Millington said,

"Okay, so, the next activity is a name game! You have to say your name, as well as all of the ones said before you. It's a harder one, I know."

Maralyn failed in two tries, then departed school that day quickly to binge a new show.

"Helena's Skin"

The next day–in the same class.

There was a stillness, after the shuffling around and readjustments at everybody's seats. Mr. Allen sat calmly, contemplating behind a silent star, yet still carrying an edge on his face. The classroom tv turned on. Somebody loudly sighed.

"Remember to get your permission slips in for the Pinegrove Exchange Day next Thursday! 15 students are needed, so please talk to Mr. Reed if you're interested." Mr. Allen said.

He nodded to himself and turned away from the students. He was there today to support Mrs. Millington in her introduction of this class.

Every table had 4 to 5 kids, a large class size given the 6 tables available. Spring humidity often combined with body heat to garner lots of wet shirt flickers and groggy, soggy faces. Although enjoyment of the renown discussions usually took care of the discomfort, the teacher made a point to start classes 5 minutes late in those months. He would also check to see if people had their water bottles ready, and if not, stop to recommend that they head out to the fountain. It served cold and clean water, as of renovation two years ago.

The announcements finished and Mr. Allen grabbed one more sip of coffee.

Maralyn's group was mainly congregated near the right side of the room, by the windows. The horizontal blinds were half down. Light and darkness coupled to send a parallelogram ray across Katrina's table and into her side. The dust made it look like a valuable mist. Maybe invaluable, to Maralyn. Her eyebrows shielded sparkles surrounded by brown and green mountains.

The girl at the opposite table looked down when she spotted the glimmer.

"She looks so beautiful," Maralyn intuitively realized but did not put into words.

She noticed others in their area peaking tiny looks in the direction of the motionless girl. Katrina might have had consciousness about such things, but it was always hard for others to tell.

Maralyn began ironically yet seriously singing, gently, "What Makes You Beautiful" by One Direction.

Their friends, but not Maralyn, noticed Katrina's cheeks suddenly blush into a pink-red, her chin covered by the shirt she began to use as a shield. They were confused by that awkward, escaping cover. Maralyn simply scratched it away, as if her friend's beauty did not and had never happened, as if it did not and would never feel right. Confusion was her new seat.

As if! This wasn't happening.

"Alright, alright," Mr. Allen commanded, standing at the front. He could tell that a few of his favorite students were growing preoccupied. With "teenage drama" or something.

Josiah and Maralyn let out very bored sighs when class officially began. Bored less because of the setting and more because of their lives. The girl sprawled her fingers like an instantly growing (terrifying) spider over Josiah's left hand. When she saw that he cutely smiled, she moved it down to his left knee and did the same, to which he slapped her hand. It was just audible enough for Mrs. Millington to notice.

Maralyn and Josiah burst out laughing, Heather joining in even though she didn't know why she was. When Mr. Allen shot them each a look, Heather faked a frown, but still glared at them as if to say: shut the fuck up, the our favorite is speaking.

He commenced the course introduction by walking around the clearing, beginning a semi-speech. He displayed delicate yet heavy reflection towards each sentence, each syllable, and the class admired him all the more for it.

The room was patient. He went on, truly starting, "You guys have been taking these Project courses, for what, months now, or even years for some of you,"

He looked down. A laughing smirk.

"And you've been in high school for longer, or maybe just as long if you're anything like Madison,"

He looked at her, so then everyone else did. Madison, a 14 year old whose schedule was nearly 3 years above her age's average, nervously giggled. Everyone turned around to look at the half-black, brown-eyed girl sitting in her spot in the back. Maralyn smiled at her, and they confidently locked eyes.

Trust. Maralyn immediately thought.

Mr. Allen kept a warm smile intact. Respect and anticipation in the air meant the day's parabolic peak. And it would often be like this. The journey of a day in his classroom. One had to be messed up or sleeping to not enjoy his guidance.

Maralyn even caught that a new face was in their Middleton class. A 5'6" girl with dirty blonde highlights added to frizzy wavy hair; calm demeanor, on her phone the entire time, two apples on top of her backpack. It looked like she had tried to eat one but stopped, probably because of one of Mrs. Millington's evil little glances. The girl reminded Maralyn of walking in or out of a movie theatre, clutching popcorn and a dark safety.

After practically burning their eyes staring at the clock here, Maralyn and her friends excitedly got up when they noticed the magic of the clockwork.

It was lunchtime, and Rosie had new packs of Marlboro Reds.

"You know," Josiah told his best friend and partner in also the Videos. "It's nice that they included this, compared to regular schools that only have grades and extracurriculars, but nobody gives a shit about our actual work,"

Maralyn felt worried suddenly.

He added, "And I was just reading the manual. What

the fuck does artistically proficient mean?"

"I completely agree," Heather told him solemnly.

"If Basquiat went here, they'd give him a C- for his little drawing, slash, poster things because they were too messy, or they're anti-American or some shit. As if the teachers know anything about politics and history. I don't know,"

The group of three chuckled at that.

"But Josiah. The three elements of a secure career after high school are Volunteering, grades, and Creativity. And the standardized exams," Maralyn said.

"Right." Heather responded, adding cynically, "Even though grades are the most important."

It was lunchtime, though. No more worries–no more pain. They were going to McDonald's.

Chapter 12

Our little boy sits watching. The eyes zoom in from behind his head to the screen. It is large now. We see inside.

"Maralyn, Maralyn, Maralyn."

What? she begins to think, bothered.

In a tone more serious now: "Don't you know you can't do that?"

Pause. Silent.

"They won't let you,"

There is a crack of innocence born from ignorance, in Ms. Genevieve's voice. The screen fizzles in white noise for the rest.

You Weren't There, So I Lost Myself Instead

Reclining at home.

It's a little strange. Really strange, Maralyn thought.

Open your eyes a little, she wish she could respectfully tell Josiah, referring to their artistic journey.

She sat in her room writing and thinking.

"Do the ideas just flow out of the skin underneath my fingertips? What is supposed to flow like metallic blood leaking from my gums? All I see is red, all I can remember is horrible childhood trips to the dentist."

I miss her. And I miss her. I'll always miss her, I miss her more and more, every day,

The missing person's flimsy jackets and black cargo pants deflected, through a prism that only seemed like a mirror to Maralyn. The pictures moved fast; luxurious cars racing on a freshly paved road in a clean-smelling city. The kids at Sigma. Their expensive graphic shirts and parents and approval and signed forms.

She looked at her face with finality.

"Take it all,"

"Take it all from me,"

The realizations of not thinking, it never occurred to her. Anyways, Maralyn decided to think about her video instead. Images, Wikipedia, references, oscillation, isolation. Yearning, pining, reaching.

She realized that she had seen all of her ideas thus far before, somewhere. In her mindfield, old journals, wall. She simply took them and ran with it. An artist's lust to create something brand new which simultaneously honored tradition and various cultures. The lust was mad, almost sick, and had-to-be-fulfilled-or-at-least-followed. Then, she remembered the work of J Dilla, and the Jim Morrison on her wall, and Ian Connor and Lana del Rey; Internet icons, cultural gods, nondescript effigies who once had childhoods. She connected to her speakers and shuffled The Beatles, then mustered up the energy to go to her desk. She began a long night of work on the video; she'd manifest concepts by scrolling through color filters and fonts, splicing the shots of Josiah's sitting down and hunched over, connecting A to B to C to B.

Two days later.

Maralyn had gotten two slices local pizza for lunch before it. She scurried to class because the walk took so long.

"So, how are you? How was everybody's little break?"

Before anyone could properly make up an answer, a stuffed Maralyn stumbled into the room, her heavy backpack on.

Mrs. Millington turned around towards the door, and: "Woah!"

The interjection was impassioned, maybe even the pinnacle of anxiety, frightening a few kids up from their comas.

"Woah," the girl lowly, sarcastically doubled back. She then stretched out her arms, in an awkward consoling-yet-scared way.

"Well, would you look at that." the teacher force-kindly said. Her eyes were full of red-orange disdain. "Young lady, you almost gave me a heart attack!"

Millington's uber forced laugh made the spotlight on Maralyn's chest burn more. Her next steps seemed darkened, making it difficult for her to turn to her seat. She remembered that Josiah would be at their table and it motivated her to look up. Although, she looked for his eyes and could not find them.

Dumbass, Jay thought about M.

When she finally "found" her seat, she intensely rolled her eyes and flopped her backpack down, for whoever to still stare at, and chugged from her disposable water bottle.

Rosie rose her eyebrows, chuckling at her, in sympathy and so she would calm down.

"Anyways," the 60-something woman said shortly. "What we're doing today, as I said we would, is watching a few videos on the history of film. They'll discuss from Edwin S. Porter and the highly influential D.W. Griffiths all the way to Quentin Tarantino and Steven Spielberg.

"Just please remember to pay attention. All of this will be very beneficial for you, in the ways you style your work and learn about yourself in the process."

Throughout the class, Maralyn's stomach (or something nearby it) grumbled–embarrassing her. She tried stifling it by hunching over or shoving her fist into the area. For the last 26 minutes of class, she listened to Nirvana through her headphones.

"Man, goodness." Maralyn began to vent about her weird bump-in with Millington, the subject everybody wanted to think and talk about together, at the end. "That was weirddd,"

"Right?" Josiah responded. "She was like, so mean to you." He breathily giggled. "You didn't even do anything,"

It somewhat bothered Maralyn that Jay was hesitantly laughing while talking about it. But she didn't put words into it because it didn't seem like a big deal. Her main thought was simply, Aren't you supposed to be defending me to the core right now? I wanted to die up there,

Rosie was nodding her plump head throughout this, eating pomegranate seeds one by one.

"Right–I know, like," Maralyn returned. "What the fuck was I supposed to do? I walked in late, so what. I don't think I look that much like an alien,"

But then an anxious daze set in. She let her friends go back and forth about it and school things and lunch plans and nicotine acquisitions.

She thought: I mean, my nose is kind of elongated, my eyes dark and pointing downwards. Am I really that ugly? Do I look that Arab? I don't know. Fuck.

Her suffocating, silent moment was interrupted by Josiah grabbing her arm, signaling to the door. It was time for lunch.

"We decided to go to White Castle," he muttered. "Come on, let's go."

Chapter 13

"They be wondering where I be at,
Boy, somewhere that you'll never get"
–Bones - TheyNeverSeemToLearn

Not by the force of an ultimate electric event does the transfer from the big screen to the cellular program happen. It occurs after months of developing and countless futile scrolls by anxious fingers.

Well. Although the boy isn't prepared for being broadcasted to a larger, more immediate audience. He has to have it.

Growing. Humanity. Reaching.

4th period history class, with Mr. Willis. Strolling around, wasting time, together as they were supposed to deliver a letter to Ms. Hortz. The nonchalant trio had a hard time finding the room in the first place. Katrina walked in front of Christina who was next to Maralyn. The wooden floor's dust was pungent as they brushed through.

"Oh my gosh, Katrina," Christina boasted in her characteristically high-pitched, scratchy voice. "Your new jacket is so pretty,"

Maralyn wouldn't have called it "pretty," but rather rustically elegant. Cowboyish, in a good way, and futuristic. It was a one of a kind brown leather jacket, accentuated with navy-grey silk patches on the sleeves and back. It was worn down yet still looked new, unique leather strips hanging near the chest and hem. Lined with magenta cotton, it insulating very well.

Katrina always had comfortable clothing on, even if it was from eBay or thrifted. She didn't wear hand-me-downs from her older brother since he was gone for college and she felt bad going through his clothes.

"Mm. Thank you, thank you," Katrina replied.

Maralyn chimed in, she hadn't said much until then. "That true goth cowboy aesthetic," she muttered. Everybody giggled, so much so that it was hard to hear Katrina's next words.

"You see? I love this big horse,"

"Aw, I love you too," Maralyn replied.

An energy of awkwardness equally flowed through the group at the gut. The sensation immediately poisoned Maralyn's ability to jest, trapping her in her tracks. Maybe it wasn't so equal.

"No," Katrina hesitated in a low voice. "I said,

"Oh. I thought you said 'I love you because,'"

"No," she said with quite forced laughter.

"You are a true cowgirl," Christine rapidly blurted out.

That's my joke, Maralyn thought.

Not realizing it, she now had an intense desire to get to this classroom and think about hanging out with Josiah after school today. To simply get lost.

Unbeknownst to them, their brisk, messy walk may have actually disturbed nearby classes. Whatever. The amazing, omnibenevolent Mr. Allen found them on their way to the room, discussing finals and his new two songs with them.

Afterwards, they found the class almost easily and got the job done right–knocking instead of just opening the door and smiling at the bullshitter teacher.

"I was fucked from the start"
–Wavves - "I Can't Dream"

Fuck you, and you, and fuck....*all* of you.

Were the thoughts that went through Harry's mind as he let the large camera revolve around his head. He was exasperated.

"Yeah, I like that," Henry was in the middle of saying. He couldn't be entirely sure of what the boys were saying; his brain was in a fog, pulled between ideation and real-world consequence. He didn't know what he wanted out of his video, what kind of message to convey, so his thoughts consistently remolded into doing well for a good grade. And hating the grade(s). And school. And all of the teachers or people who would grade the Projects.

"I don't fucking have time for this, dude." he told Trevor, the boy behind the camera, their main director. He was going to say "this bullshit," but didn't want to sound too girly.

"Alright man," Trevor responded, busy concentrating.

Fuck you. This is why Maralyn always hates on the school, and is a bitch to teachers. The system sucks and makes me want to die.

I don't even like our idea, he wanted to say–but didn't, couldn't, it would have very much hurt the others' (who were Trevor, Dakota, and Benny) feelings. So he maintained his gloomy straight face.

At the next turn of the camera, one where it appeared in front of his face, he flared into it–with the compulsive intensity of someone finally landing a grab of their months-long addiction. He then smiled cruelly, without regard for the type of audience in mind.

"Alright, cool," Trevor told him, chuckling and looking somewhere else. "I think we got what we need,"

Trevor realized that he would probably edit all of these things out, or just disregard the film.

That day, Henry realized something. That he wished he had a nose ring. Silver, lowkey, just something. Maybe a bigger and more embellished one in the future; for now, he simply didn't have one.

One of the props of their video was a guitar, Benny's metallic gold Fender. Henry was to pretend-play Mathew's own work in their song.

I don't even play guitar, he thought. Ridiculous and embarrassing… I don't think I can do this,

I don't even think I can make it, in their video. I can't make this. I don't know.

Drip

Josiah, walking down the curved Sigma hallway, realized that he needed to dramatically shift his course in life in order to better accommodate good friendships, letting in positivity and love.

He realize it all one step at a time, left foot gliding over right foot, from the first hallway to the one here with Maralyn. They were here for their voluntary sit-in of a Sigma Project class, touring the area before heading in.

She was in the middle of talking. His ears suddenly tuned back in.

"I've had enough of garbage people teaching us and kids doing honestly garbage things," Maralyn said.

He looked ahead, still in a daze.

Josiah! she wanted to slam to him while flicking his forehead, have you been even listening to me?

In reality, she asked him, "You feel me?"

He had been facing the windows for most of the trip. Looking; at the currently nearby bundles of bourgeoisie trees with yellow, yellow light going through them, not at anything in particular.

"What?" he turned and said. "What? Oh yeah. Yeah, I understand what you,"

No you don't, Maralyn thought immediately. "Okay, then," Her response was fragmented, unfocusing, a face turning red. She would just continue admiring the semi-foreign setting, maybe soaking it in even more.

The outdoor situation was embellished. Adjacent to

those pine and oak trees were kidney-shaped soil grounds–outlined by some sections of little, round flowers. The rest was wood chips and prickly bushes. Chrysanthemums, pink yellow and blue, were interrupted minorly by elegant tulips. The spot seemed like it smelled good from the ground rising.

Josiah had starry eyes, his visage melting in the prism of the glass. Maralyn focused on her shoes and their steps as they strolled. The adventure was random, guided by natural obedience to attractants. They only switched ways in lieu of obstacles.

If they needed to confront a teacher, an unfriendly student, a dead end, their movements would tumble. But after a few moments, they would push forward more directedly and convicted than before. Maralyn looked down at her Converses; thoughts of light creeping at her from the bottom up.

As the duo trotted along, a 5'5" black boy with a frizzy, medium-sized afro turned the corner towards them. Only Josiah truly paid attention to him. His eyes seemed sad, or just really tired, and it seemed like he always had those big headphones on.

But I don't want to make too many assumptions about this kid, Josiah thought.

A few seconds later, sun dripping into the hall as if it was holding back, the room seemed to become a standstill for Jay. He was suddenly conscious of his single eyelids and silky black hair, even recalling his grandparents' immigration from China story. His hair was long (for a boy) and wavy, but that didn't mean a thing. They came face-to-face with the boy.

When the moment was over, Jay realized something–it was as if that black boy had told Josiah something. For him, or at least something only a select few people, he included, could comprehend. Or should.

He saw the sadness again–and a darkness–but with such a core of starlight entrenched in a pinpoint inside the spirit. Whatever it was that he was supposed to understand, Josiah believed that his look back had said "I get it."

But do I really? he wondered.

The yellow and pink flowers outside shone for him, almost, making a pathway on both sides although one of them was really unattractive lockers. But, he was suddenly shook about their predicament.

"Where are we going after this? What are we doing here after we have to leave? You know, 'cause we have to get back to school and shit,"

Maralyn let out a groan-turned-sigh. She replied, "Wherever we wanna go. Have you seen this place? I'll probably just skip class."

When her friend seemed very uncomfortable at this, she laughed.

"I mean, like, what do *you* want to do?" Her tone was fast, the "to" sounding like a rough "tuh." She added, "You're so indecisive," under her breath.

"I mean like… Maralyn! I don't know! I guess I just feel like I need to get back to my calc' class soon, so I can prepare for our test. It's on Friday."

"Friday!" she exclaimed. "That's in forever. You're going to be fine,"

"Um, no, Maralyn–I don't think you get it."

He chuckled, grimacing.

Borders of defense built upon her face. Then, her weakening and shying voice replied, "Yes I do, I'm taking pre-calculus, and three days is a bunch of time to study! Plus, you always get As,"

Since it was Tuesday, she was referring to studying all day long until then. But maybe he had his own, positive, reasons for helping himself in class. They glared at each other for a few seconds, then simultaneously burst out giggling in the moderately loud (some students began to come in from lunch) East wing.

"You're a stinky, stinky…pie," he told her, their eyes locking suspiciously.

Maralyn then semi smiled. "Thanks. You are too,"

Deeet, deeet, deeet!

Lunch was officially over–the rest of the Sigma population would be pouring in–and fourth period commenced in 9 minutes.

Maralyn and Josiah didn't waste any time; they consulted the map online for where the class was, looking up at students nervously. They were being looked at as strangers, or even the true foreigners who they were. So they also looked up madly, rudely, reciprocating the energy of hostility. As youths do.

When they finally landed the correct room number, Josiah sighed in relief and Maralyn set her Maralyn near the window. She decided that she wouldn't be needing it, not interested in taking notes today. This was a momentous occasion, as they had heard much about Sigma's Project classes and fell in love with the Level A architecture today.

Going from the brightly lit, white hall into the large, wood and felt room felt portal-like. It felt as if walking through the door made one's world all black, then scanned them for dangerous possessions. And then promised to heal them of that need once sitting in the lecture.

The demeanor of the room was heavy, windy, a portrait of humanity's capability for finding both its psychological stories and potentials for formulating empowerment. And capturing, transforming, manifesting, releasing.

Undertones of classical music. And Oliver Peoples glasses and ambient music.

They were actually too shy to take a seat at first, simply peering in near the dark brown door. The place was nearly as tall as an auditorium, boxy, and narrow enough to fit four rows of pods at the back. Four of them in each row, split in halves. The two rows in the back were elevated above the others, probably for room to see the front. The front which was literally a stage. A large, high-quality projector beamed the day's objectives and due work.

These pods were cozy little white and plastic chairs, covered in glass protective layers. They completely blocked views from the other ones and the ceiling–forming a personal habitat for the student. This encouraged privacy and focus, via seclusion, but the pods were open enough for comfort and communication with teachers. The very last intention for them was preventing cheating.

And for classrooms such as these at Sigma, there were always two teachers, not one. All high-level and Project courses were in them.

The lesson began as soon as each student settled comfortably in their pods. The young male teachers, one black and one white, even waited for Maralyn and Josiah to acclimate at their guest desks. They had searched around the room for smiles and eye contact.

Shown by the projector was an ovary of boulders with flames abounding, and crackling open. It was from a supplemental video demonstrating the concept of a new world's genesis.

Mr. Hahn stood to its left and Mr. Terrance to its right. The floor was clean brown wood, surrounded by dirty orange walls. The lesson continually referenced the births of the largest religions. Maralyn and Josiah took notes furiously. They had never had a Project lesson like this, especially in the visuals. The bursting oranges and far bright, blue sky excited the girl.

Rarely checking the notes on his MacBook Air, the blond Mr. Hahn detailed the origins of Christianity.

Alongside that, Mr. Terrance began confidently, "You see,"

He was a tall black man with a short undercut and an exercised build.

Quickly turning to the screen, "They were past generations of humans *trying*. They were trying to do their best to build the right worlds for themselves. They often utilized symbols of their central figures, but the base idea was togetherness. And that's a uniting factor in almost every religion. They're ritualistic–to bring people together."

The students looked up at them as if they were the leaders of those civilizations.

Maralyn peered to her left at those pods, and then felt a somewhat pleasant, pink envy. Her and her best friend knew that these were the ones, they were the lucky kids. Positive change in her generation's world would likely be maintained by them, if not totally started. Because they had had enough time off—relief in positive spaces—to cultivate real education. Not wasting away, imprisoned, in depression and minimum wage jobs.

And the lesson soon ended after the teachers lead a short Q&A, rather than the usual Socratic seminar, pods steered into a circle–because they wanted to formally introduce Maralyn and Josiah to the class.

"Why, hello, lovely everyone." Maralyn announced pleasantly.

To Have A Platform

The next day.

Maralyn decided to idle the day away at school, finishing a French project inside each class she was in. Later on, she joined Rosie, Jesse, and Brett at the forest, smoking out of small bong. Her phone received two buzzes as they walked around their spot. The vibrations felt urgent but not important. The lock screen showed that they were from Josiah. Maralyn opened them up.

°dont u just love it when people complain about mental illness via cynical jokes on social media, while making zero effort to combat these problems. in real life and to actually recover°

°hahaha i fucking love it°

Maralyn chuckled, with confused eyebrows. She agreed. She pulled the screen closer to her eyes and began typing rapidly: °Oh yes, I love it° °Especially when they waste my time and not contribute anything positive°

Pursing her dry lips, she warily looked around at her friends. Nobody noticed it or cared that she took to her phone. Brett was great in particular at recognizing paranoia and stifling his own.

°u dig? u feel?° °fuck those kids.°

She suddenly became out of breath.

°Yes, i somewhat feel you°

And that was the end of that for now. She trusted that Jay was okay. Her group strolled around for 10 minutes before retreating to Brett's cozy car.

Katrina's Silver Hammer

°human bones, hUman sKuLL° was the caption of an Instagram photo Katrina saw earlier, by Jordan, her photographer friend who went to Middleton.

They had met in a painting class in her freshman year, he was a year older. Jordan often posted pictures to Behance, a photography sharing website with an underground usership. He still used Instagram to find commissions and connections, but cynically, with joke, absurd, or cryptic language. He rarely shared his face. Katrina always made sure to consider that he was black when she judged his work.

She would remember his short, lanky figure, and love it–but rarely felt warmth towards him. She thought that it was due to the coldness of his art. There was still trust.

"Well you know my ego has been dead," Katrina was telling Maralyn. "For the past like, seven months,"

And then she chuckled.

Is it? Maralyn wondered.

Truthfully, she just wanted to hold Katrina's face for a little while. She didn't really care about her ego or id or consciousness or state of mind at the moment. But she didn't know that, Maralyn hadn't processed any of these truths.

"Yeah." Maralyn responded.

"Yeah," Katrina chuckled back.

Katrina looked into Maralyn's eyes and saw the image of an Instagram profile with its several notifications at the bottom or a scroll of Tweets rapidly updating.

They were in Katrina's basement, studying for tests– which was usually a peaceful, nondramatic event. Friends would gather in her cold yet homey little sanctuary and devour whatever snacks were in the house. "I share my food unlike white people," she once said, eliciting long laughter from Maralyn.

Back.

How am I supposed to do this? M thought.

And then the sun shone into the room, and she remembered the recent moons as well. They simultaneously did an awkward shift to different sides of their butts on the seats.

How did I get here?

Over the seconds, Katrina felt this unexplained, irrational urge to glare into her friend's eyes. Hold onto them for a second. If there is a God, she thought, he might help me figure this all out,

Before I get guilty… No, I won't leave here with her making me guilty. Maybe I'll walk to the parking lot with her. But she won't ever have an...unjust, nonsensical hold on me. Even though she always wants to hug me before going and wonder about my male interests. No, not Maralyn.

Maralyn saw her friend's current status as just being cold. And she did actually walk away abruptly. It was as if she forgot that Maralyn was even there.

I find it really funny how much, and how often she wants to be around me, but does things that make that from happening the complete opposite, Katrina continued to think. Like… just completely negating the opportunity of all that.

You know, I know I'm stuck in this simulation,

This simulation of love and happiness and mutual joy, she thought. Maralyn, you didn't make it possible; you didn't make it happen. These thoughts had been interrupted by her mother, yelling at her from downstairs to clean the kitchen for her friends. "Depression & Obsession" by XXXTentacion had just come on too, probably Christina, and she tried quickly yelling to the Alexa to change the song. Likely, only her mother heard that.

When her intelligence resurfaced, she heard Maralyn say "I'm here with you," in her mind. It elicited confused yet joyful emotions, the whole experience foreign.

But she doesn't even talk to me like a real person! Or look at me like one,

I'm just a hurt person, she thought, almost two minutes after Maralyn thought: I've been through a lot as a person.

When Maralyn got home that night, she came to an ugly, twisted realization. She had been staring at her messages, wondering why Katrina never texted first to meet up or say hi, or even send memes. Nothing. She thought: her friendship, affection, and appreciation don't exist because she never sent them.

Oh well, she thought before getting into bed, at least we got an A on our Project Paper,

Chapter 14

The next day. Thursday. The walk from the lot had been hushed–hiding a tri-colored light in a bag. Multiple bags. The emotions which came out when one opened them were too earthshattering for the Opifer building to handle.

Wobbling. Dakota steadied his descentings with a grasp on another's arm, and the younger group found it very amusing. Of course, Maralyn chuckled, but she zoomed past the clump because she had something to do.

Or, thought that she did.

For years, since moving to the area and maybe because of more happenings, Jay told himself that he would never stop for reckless abandoning, especially by haughty men or drunken girls. He wouldn't go out of his way to comfort them, and if they were causing a publicized nuisance, he would probably tell on them. To teachers, cashiers, waitresses, and lastly police, whatever authority figure was nearby. Lurking by, a heavy uncertainty guided him as he glared their way from the lockers across from them.

The bigger kids' torsos let out a sweet, sweat aroma. Dakota's back was clearly extremely drenched. And they might have been vaping before coming. This contributed to the fruity and uppity aura around them. At a certain point, Maralyn walked out of her classroom nearby and stalled by her friends.

Mr. Willis personally couldn't tell if the boys in the group were drunk, high, or both. In any case, he backed out of the area. With a secret hope in mind that a more strict teacher would take care of them. If there needed to be taking care of.

Well, I'll just be going now, he reasoned–masking the affectionate politeness he felt inside or liked to feel–you know what to do!

Oh boy, Katrina thought after she arrived in the hall with Trevor.

Dakota and Jordan began to wildly jump in unison. The tall, thick boys clapped their hands onto one another's and shoved other boys around with their big shoulders. Masking their loud intentions was a drag.

"Oh my, oh my," the Trevor and Katrina cringingly mumbled over the song playing from somebody's speaker.

Then Brett joined, and so did several others, "I've been up for a long time, broad day!"

Maralyn snickered to herself, mouthing the lyrics alongside them while beaming at Jordan and Jesse.

Henry had a hold on the speaker and incrementally turned up the volume. The whole hall was a buzzing cauldron of bodies bobbing and teenagers overjoyed with unintentionally scandalous behavior.

Katrina's eyes had in them a marveling glow that turned from side to side. "You are insane," she spoke. She nearly shut her eyes with a shy head squirm which she did when she was too giddy about something. Too many good feelings. Maralyn always thought that it was the cutest thing.

It was getting warmer outside, and these were the memories many of them would end up saving. Unbeknownst to them, as well as all-too-forgetful teachers, because the little event would definitely be shut down soon. In the spontaneous haste, Rosie's group of girls felt a little paranoid. Not pure paranoia, but a feeling of displacement. Or, almost displacement. Rosie and Katrina had been fidgeting, clutching onto their backpack lapels or biting fingernails. Observing them, Josiah thought they had been getting rid of these annoying habits and were getting better, "but I guess I didn't know." And for him, Katrina, and Heather, the boys seemed like posers, ignoring not only them but current cultural issues in light of popping music. Plus, Josiah was upset for people who had music tastes outside of rap.

Although she wanted to dive into those kids' inviting black sun, Jesse was searching for a slow jam. In life and sound. At every turn those weeks, she saw only Max's eyes under male brunette fade cuts, scanning boys' Under Armor garments for strong arms like his. And with every reminder or match, her entire being cringed. Then, she would tentatively leave her station early in order to go fantasize about him some more and properly. The gathered vision board would be sufficient for filling the hole so cruelly left inside of her.

Getting the mail was too hard of a task for these kids, hungover or sober, so how would impromptu dance parties be unified? Besides simply watching. Or waiting for teachers to finally come bust it–the entire hallway's energy going up in flames. Ashes, and then again until a group the next year, and again.

Katrina's awkward sighs, tethered to thoughts like "All I can hear right now is Henry saying some shit like 'Party, baby, party,'" were heard by a lord down under. While the result wasn't what she had been hoping for, the pressure gave.

Something gave.

Like soft, sinister, white smoke, Middleton's principal Mr. Beaman alongside Mr. Ryedigger rushed in as quickly as a new elevator.

Ding! Swoosh.

"*Turn* that off!" they both nearly simultaneously screamed. They screeched more commands into Jordan and Brett's ears.

When the entire collective paused in inaction or unwillingness, Mr. Ryedigger's face turned tomato red. Maralyn had to hold back a chuckle because his neck was beginning to inflame too, a horrendous mixture of blotched yellow, Florida-tan orange, pink, and blood red.

"What?" Dakota whimpered weakly, only half-rhetorically. "Why?"

The principal swatted into the crowd's openings, as if the music and noises were flies.

"Uh-uh, not appropriate," he clamored in response to one of the boy's pleading.

By that time, the speaker was already off and being stored.

"We're going to figure out what to do about this." he said.

Josiah grumbled.

"Here we fucking go." Trevor quietly muttered.

Deet! On.

A junior boy from Sigma presented himself.

His aura was like black and white. But black and white were just lazy versions of nothing. His presence was clear lightning to the murky, hazy vortex like the kids' lives.

And when he stepped in that day, it was like a satisfying breeze of fresh air.

"You know that none of this is real, right?" he said–when he saw Maralyn and a few underclassmen gluing their eyes to the bright boards. "You know it's not real."

And Maralyn responded by turning up at him with deeply tired, and troubled, eyes, and saying, "I'm almost done; I promise I'm almost done here,"

With a devious near-smile. As if honey and not glue was guiding her throat.

Her hands even seemed purple at the backs with their strain, as well as decaying and dry. But she did take his advice.

If these are my demons, she thought while analyzing Katrina's new hairstyle, and they are going to kill me, I don't care. I don't know what else to do,

I didn't know what to do.

As if defending herself against an already questioning enemy–who was omnipotent.

Logging out, as well as out of her Twitter and Tumblr, felt like ripping off parts of herself. The last thing she saw was a Tweet from Sage: °Let me provide, bc you know I do this hoe°

And. Later–after he had left and the young students cleared and Mrs. Wilson the librarian, let the late-rides people use the computers–Maralyn logged back on expediently. The girl savored the fruits of cameras everywhere, on everybody. A camera actually, one camera. "The human race" she had labeled it.

But maybe, labeling things isn't always a good thing, she remembered Katrina telling her once.

And the label was wrong. She felt it, and knew it, but still used it to justify herself as learning more about her girl, schoolwork, and ultimately herself.

Making connections, stalking profiles (including "the boy's"), saving dozens of data a day, forgetting context and clocks.

Chapter 15

Flower…Fever

Later on. Somewhere.

"Dakota,"

Her voice sounded like a flower.

He blushed and then smiled at her. "What?"

The room was abuzz with fresh food and the energy of ubiquitous phones. Rosie smiled with the knowledge that they were surrounded by good actors and stimuli. Mainly, her soul was at peace in his spirit's arms' embrace.

He grinned back, but maybe even grimacing inside.

The junior and senior pair strolled around the house, stumbling.

Chick ching.

"Dynamite with a laser beam"
–Queen - Killer Queen

The channel was on an arbitrary number, plus the resolution not at its maximum. But this was all to reset the system so that it would stream faster.

He had discovered special silence–a static, steady energy–in that electronic realm.

"Increase the noise," the boy says, clearly and powerfully. "Please,"

He thought of Katrina's gorgeous face next, and was angry. His face was angry and full of something to say t–.

You mean so much to me, she thought but didn't say.

Oh, you really do,

Katrina peered up at him steadily, adoring his eyes and hands and choice of socks for the day.

The thought, "miss me with that bullshit," went through his head then.

Giving Form Again and Again

"I was transfixed with her body and style, a continual smile growing on my face. Like it felt when I first heard the group play and we made songs together. If I could tell you everything, if I could tell you exactly what I remember, it would be benefit the both of us so much. I really would; you'd learn a lot and everything. But it's hard to articulate,"

The boy nods.

She types into her phone notes,

"Instead of falling
Slipping
Into, away
into, away
The best I can be, is
Everything"

"Come on; take it back for me. Bring it back, to me, to you."

Maralyn stares intently at him.

"Yes, Maralyn. I'm pushing you."

She stares on. His deep voice, with that.

She swallows.

"I see you're not ready." he tells her.

"It's not complicated. It's not a formal or business issue,"

"You don't have to deal with it like that, Maralyn,"

But she is already looking away. Still sitting towards him, her entire upper body twists towards a tall window. Into the sunlight, fantasizing a future about Katrina's eyes.

The next day; at Opifer.

The vents were on high (power). The steel tunnels in the ceiling blasted cold air all around. The pair turned a sharp corner, from a humid room into a dark amber hallway to a cream one. They were in an obscure Sigma hallway system.

Mr. Allen said quietly, "Come on down."

He opened a bulky door, it had a shiny and silver handle. The teacher led them down the stairs. Maralyn wouldn't remember much from this afterwards besides the temperature of that stairwell. Her huffs could almost produce clouds. While she was walking through, though, she was wary about the place's quietness. It was inverted and almost dead. But she wouldn't remember feeling scared. Mr. Allen was nearby; there was nothing to fear. Much of her faith as simply a human being in the schools had been counseled by his guidance, for three years now; she was curious about the odd excursion. Their hands slid the railings on the way to a secluded room on the new floor. His brown hands showed wrinkles and dark blue veins.

As Mr. Allen led the way, Maralyn's black Vans squeaked. The walkway seemed too long and insecure, like a narrow highway. It was also the power of the dim, old LEDs, mixed in with pure white walls. Maralyn felt energy creep out of her, out of her fingertips to the stomach. After a minute of nervously looking left and right, she swiped out her phone. She mindlessly scrolled on an app which rarely had service in the school's uncommon areas.

Mr. Allen turned lightly to check on his apprentice. Instantly, his face was pinkish at the sight.

"Young lady!"

The loud calling interrupted the tranquilizing quiet they had been working on for (almost) half an hour. His tone was not condescending, but the voice still naturally coarse.

Maralyn, confident in her boredom, very slowly looked up from the iPhone.

"Yea?"

The walls took on a redder hue behind their eyes. Neither of the two caught the digital clock hanging from the crusty ceiling above. That was probably for the better. They probably would have noticed three red numbers blaring at them in a harsh artificial light. Two different people with varying goals in mind, but both would have been agitated about the time it was. The anger would have been rooted in true desire to go home and get work done, or lie on a coach half-numb and half-receptive to distracting tv or music.

"You are so distracted, my God," he cried.

The girl, putting her phone back in her coat pocket, said, "It just feels like we've been down here forever, and I don't know where we're going," Even when she tried not to, she hesitated. "and yeah,"

"I have important things to show you," he responded. "I feel like if you go on your phone, it'll interrupt all your attention,"

At this, Maralyn felt a twinge, a physiological response to something her mind immediately found ridiculous. It was almost miraculous. What does my phone have to do with it? she thought.

She told him, willfully but with as much respect as possible, "I'm still paying attention,"

"No, no, no," with a calm authoritative voice. "You aren't mentally present during the current task if you keep going on your phone out of nowhere. Just saying! Statistics, science, are proving it every day,"

"I realize that..." There was objection, hidden at the tiny cracks of her inflection. But, their relationship was too valuable to tarnish with debates (arguments) about commonplace influences. The burnt wall hues still ultimately favored conflict. "I'm sorry," she said, drawing out the y. Meaning it.

The next day. There could have been clouds. There could have been rain falling from up over them, and they could have thought of looking for umbrellas. This was what passing through the Mystery Floor did to them. They had their time for choice. If the world wanted to be confusing, it would be.

This was right here. Nothing was going to start, begin, build. Nothing was going to resume, and this was never going to end.

The two were in the library, and their hands were respectively in engagement. The room was fact, it was truth in their present moment. Truth forever; Mr. Allen knew that, Maralyn was beginning to.

"Remember what it is?" Mr. Allen asked, holding up a complementary bookmark that he had picked up from the front desk.

Your Words Have an Impact On Me is what it boldly stated in purple against a light mustard yellow background. A brown little girl with wide eyes and an O mouth was on it, staring out at them.

Maralyn wanted to speak but almost couldn't. She reached out to touch the girl's face. It did not remind her of anything. There were no words for all of this, any of it.

"I talked about it in class one day, but I guess you don't remember,"

Maralyn shyly looked towards the table.

There could have been clouds, but there wasn't. Clean white stars in their eyes magnified everything that was going on.

"You're a savage of the truth," she slowly thought, about her other teacher, in fragments.

What about the pain of children? That was something she had written underneath a drawing one time.

Mr. Allen started on the bookmark. Adults nearby were talking about the novel *Infinite Jest*.

Maralyn was patient. The moment was ready. The mood lightened again.

"Most people have a bookshelf at home. Not that most of them use them," quickly laughing, "but they're a great thing to have. I know you're a real reader, and so am I. Now try to imagine somebody, some crazy witch, or capitalism or something, comes by and destroys your entire collection. That diverse, rich, meaningful part of your life is destroyed."

"Okay," Maralyn said.

"Imagine your entire library is one single book. It's the pot of gold, the marker of cascades of emotions and developments that you took on one day when you decided to read it. Your bookmark, this bookmark, is that evil person, that force. Putting this slip in there is calm, chill, chill as you guys say, steady and binding force. It is a block to your progress as a reader and as a person. The longer you keep waiting to pick it up, slowly decreasing the need for it, the more that gets destroyed. Does that make sense?"

"Yes, yes it does,"

"While holding off on finishing the book and relying on your brain to store the memories, your awareness becomes blanker and blanker. Soon you might not even remember the essential things, leaving you at a blank slate, as before you started reading and collecting. The memory of the bookshelf will still be there, but there is no content. Wobbly memory only, no substance. You understand? You can't read from the memory of a bookshelf."

Pause.

He chuckled, "You might even be too traumatized from the sight of the flaming destruction to even get up and try again! Because some part of you will know how important that was. That original memory, that journey in the present moment. Don't be lazy, kiddo."

And that was the magic of Mr. Allen. His talk was the push of the bright yellow sphere inside of a space all horizontal and grey-black.

"The longer you wait to finish something important and good, the more the world comes for it and what you hold most precious,"

Maralyn had been sweating a little bit and never once looked away from the man. His crinkled cheeks seemed glimmery and freshly sculpted underneath his eyebrow hoods and the fluorescent lighting. Allen's eyes had been set in a lowered, ethereal gaze.

"It's kind of paradoxical because when something is good, you don't want it to finish," Maralyn told him.

"Not necessarily, like with higher effort activities, such as reading. But it is a paradox. You can enjoy a book so much, yet love laziness. Or be accustomed to it, rather. Love excuses even more. And so other thrills and entertainment take its place, because it's quicker, it's instant. Yet it's passive, and so, so fleeting."

"Excuses are forever," she told him, laughing.

"Dang right they are."

For us young people anyway, she thought next. And when she did, he said, "I don't blame you. I mean you've heard it all before, but you guys have it differently. I don't blame you,

"There is a ridiculous amount of expectation for you kids. And even average results are at such a high cost. You're one of the most mentally ill and depressed generations yet. I don't know how we haven't eased up on you yet. And, yet, still: it's up to y'all to rise up and change things.

"Things are even harder for kids in low-income areas. How do you reach them? And how do *they* reach the legislation and standards that they don't agree with?"

"Right." Maralyn said–her frizzy Arab hair accentuated right now.

"Middleton kids, as you and I know, have a different experience from Sigma kids. There are these discrepancies, when college application and graduation time comes around, that the world at large needs to pay attention to."

"Oh I completely agree, Mr. Allen," she replied. Smiling, "We'll get it all figured out. I promise you,"

He looked at her with an understanding similar to taking someone's two hands for a moment. The sun flickered through the clouds, giving sparkle to the sparse snow outside.

Their moment was soon over.

Chapter 16

"im worse at what
i do best
and for this gift,
i feel blessed"
–Nirvana - Smells Like Teen Spirit

Encircling.

Enraptured.

Katrina looks blankly into the camera. She has found it out. She has reached aware–

The screen fuzzles, as it does when it rains or the connection becomes hindered for some reason. She has found us out!

17. 100. 21, 22. 420. 6. 7. 17. 18. 9. 19. 20.

Encircling. Encircling. Enraptured. Encrypted. Encircling. Encircling.

The ambience of the stuck programming rested/rests at a perfect 20 out of 50 on the/her device's volume scale.

Her hands want to expand. Her long, pianoly fingers desire to, uh, stretch out, unwind from the middle knot or expectations that may have trapped them.

She is an artist. She is a jazz song.

Nobody cares about her, truly.

The girl "is" nothing. She looks like…they want her to be the evil. The scary darkness–it could germinate inside of her. She has so much self control. That is why people trust her. For she will not release, let go. The darkness will not escape her, it will not enter her. It will never! Her womb is eternal, anarchic.

She does not have red hair, amber or orange or stop sign. What she does have was light dark eyes, a narrow nose; some things enough to touch her, imagine her, control her, abuse her, die inside of her, without actually knowing her. Hahaha, ironic. Paradoxical. Symbology. The study of the English language in all its syntax, grammar, parts.

"Just ask me if I believe in God, already," she pleads to the stupid motherfucking little black and transparent camera. All these questions, she thinks. "I'm not a mystery, and I'm not evil,"

"For fuck's sake," she mutters while walking down the beige hallway with baby blue tiles.

Unravel the language. Every interaction is an interview. We are all–

"I can't believe what they did to her." she knows Maralyn has said at some point. "…I participated."

°im dead inside° Katrina thinks of Tweeting.

Sirens, ringing bells, Christmas! It is not.

She does not know what is inside of her. Christmas, ringing, bells. Spongebob Squarepants.

There is no imagery or visual comfort or marketing campaign. Or diffusers or leather massage beds or ASMR or Mediterranean air. It is not Christmas; he is not there. There was–

Suddenly the crumpling of paper sounds. Maybe, it reverberates in the waves between the two girls. Just maybe, it is that, that comfortable used paper; that is them. Or? Illuminated, by a amber and cedarwood candle. They are losing connection, though.

They are becoming out of touch. They are "losing signal."

Maralyn thinks now.

I can't believe they used her like that.

She thinks.

My cherub. My cherry blossom. My flower, my honey, my stuffed animal.

As much as I fucking hate to say it.

My everything. Somehow. The bottom of a well. Down under. Thoughts become nothing. Like Frank Ocean songs become memories. Death, dying, pigmentation, prejudice, rape, I am not okay–can you tell?

Fucking hell.

I'm not okay. Without you, without her, without anyone. How did we get...from A to B? Katrina.

The one who makes me feel like a kid, but all grown up. That one. The rain, the poetic device, the metaphor. The one who makes me feel anything. The one who has the potential to stretch, and grow, becoming everything. The big apple that I, we, every single one of us, bites into because we are obsessed. We do not bite because of her, we bite her. We are thirsty. Very.

Veeerrrryyyyy.

Mother Nature is here! We are surrounded. We're supposed to be mates. Playmates. But the substances, the commodities, the gentrification, the governments–

"They distracted me from my baby… My angel." she announced.

Your drugs. Your politics. They will never work on me. Rock and punk!

I am so sorry, you strange, perfect girl. For everything of mine You mean everything to me,

And more. I could never really put into words, or at least coherent and rational ones, all of this, and I still cannot. It's still like this.

I promise you–anything you want, I will be there for you. To have it. With it. Be it. *Think* of it and I will transport to your side with it.

> You've given me a reason to breathe, and see; the
> form being "once more." My form, yours. To love.
> "Freak!" Once more.

The next day.

Kids coming in and out of Mr. Willis' 4th period.

It was a study day, aka play music from laptops or talk about society day.

"Remember what it was like to actually care about a social cause?" Josiah asked Maralyn lowly.

"Hahahaha," she replied. "Gentrification, boy, gentrification got me fucked up."

I don't even know who I am anymore these days–am I real? she then thought.

Maralyn spoke abruptly then, but so was Josiah.

"Well… That's a social cause," he replied.

Hmph, she thought.

"Yeah, you're right. That's smart."

He wished that she would explain what she meant–but it would probably be futile. Her words had been an irrational, wacky mess lately, especially during long monologues or rants.

But what does that mean? Josiah thought. And…where is it coming from?

"I don't know, just liiike–" she said while stretching. As if she had read his mind. "White peopllee. White people, bro. You know. They got me fucked up,"

After an uncomfortable pause, "No, no, I don't really know,"

Tender, a junior girl with a soothing presence, had been surveying the conversation (whilst eavesdropping). She was black. Entering it now, "I completely relate to that, Maralyn."

Then Josiah quickly responded, hesitatingly, "Okay. I can understand that,"

Maralyn was glad to have a real audience now. She turned around to Tender and spoke as if giving a speech.

"You know, like, how social justice and activism are trends now–it's a big thing to care about minorities and people of color and stuff, and being into caring about black people's issues and communities and history,"

Josiah understood what she was going for, and for the most part agreed. He nodded throughout, saying little yeahs to move her forward.

"That's kinda what gentrification is, that's what it does," further, "People who do not belong in a specific area or sphere, going ahead and offering their opinions, and changing things. About things they genuinely don't understand inside. And then the actual people affected have to pay for certain bad decisions or unthought-out or ignorant things,

"You know what I mean? Ha! And like we'll have to explain why something or someone is bad, like let's say microaggressions, and they're more mad about the topic than us. Because they want to understand so badly but they never have and never will," She concluded with, "That's why white people got me fucked up. Do you know what I mean?"

"Yes, girl. I feel you," Tender responded in her deep, prickly voice, laughing.

"I understand what you're saying, Maralyn" Josiah responded. "But, don't you think that they're trying to learn? Like trying to be less ignorant,"

Isn't Katrina white? he wanted to say.

"No because if the intentions were there, if they were in that good place, there wouldn't be such a thing as gentrification–none of this would be a problem, everybody would be working towards fighting bigotry with a pure heart. But that's not how it is."

She nervously paused, looking to Tender. The girl nodded, in deep thought.

"A lot of people are in it for the social perks, and social acceptance even in some cases, and just looking like a good person. Online and what not, on their Instagram or Twitter profiles, or for school, just appearing virtuous,"

Josiah and Maralyn's auras were connected by the sticky tension of their recent friendship hiccups, this conversation contributing to it. The topic was important, however, they both realized that, and the fresh feeling of "starting again one day" kept them in place.

He knew that she was completely right, or at least agreed with all of it, but it was so much to take in at once. Not cryptic, yet so many messages. What am I going to do with you, girl, he thought.

"I know what you mean, Maralyn. It's going to be okay." Tender responded. "I think what black people need to do is support each other in their communities, and build coalitions in support of black businesses. And so they'll hopefully build up their own politicians, because we have like no representation. I feel you–the U.S. government is garbage and all they do, with the police, is hate black bodies."

"Right, yes. Like I completely understand what you're getting at. I totally support black-owned businesses, and the homegrown organizations that are running things–especially in disadvantaged cities,"

Then, a quirky, outspoken girl heard their loudening conversation.

Kyanna entered the D floor room, with two friends.

She was half Puerto Rican, like Katrina (making Maralyn like her even more, never noticing that their names were also similar), and the social theory, social justice type. Sort of radical, interested in Black Pantherism. Many at all of Opifer were enamored with her.

She spoke: "Okay. Can I just put in my two cents about white people? Or, I'm sorry, the majority of Americans, regular Americans, Western people, the conquerors, the colonists–whichever except white people. So I was trying to tell this dude from Sigma the other day: literally every idea you have and every Project video you make is because of our culture. It's indebted to black culture–we created everything, the memes, the dances, the music, the lyrics, the words, the social ideas, everything. Black people created pop music, rap music, jazz, funk, techno, dance, and we still do every single day. And this kid just did not understand.

"Like. What we get for it is being discriminated against when they recommend the Creative groups–all black people are automatically grouped together–or getting ignored by our teachers, being called the n-word, or them playing "Billie Jean" at homecoming. It makes us fucking uncomfortable, and little systemic change is made.

We'll get a story in the Opifer newspaper, or even the *real* local newspaper, but our administrations do little to effect change… In the students' minds, their parents', the people who actually are here and do racist things–except by name, on the surface. They just don't care, bro; but we're suffering,"

During her ideas spoken, which felt like 30 minutes but was a few, other students began to pour in. The intimate setting turned into a group, appearing like a seminar.

"Yeah. Seriously," Tender as soon as she was done, and Maralyn nodded.

A senior named Sid, who was close with Kyanna and good friends with Josiah and Sage, joined the discussion.

In his brazen yet dancey voice, he muttered, "Yeah. Like, fuck y'all talking about character education? We are the characters and the education. You don't do shit,"

Every person in the room laughed.

The mood was still somber–where a few kept silent to connect ideas, while the talkative students survived the dialogue. Maralyn had thought about this topic since she was a freshman in Opifer, and was glad to see some truth come to life. She realized that her and Josiah's Project paper could have used more direct comments such as these.

These kids, she thought, in our schools and "community," don't feel that visible. It's on the part of white or non-black people; we have been seeing them as black as their skin, camouflaged against the background. I remember I used to notice weirdly, as a kid, that a black person's face driving a car was hard to see sometimes, just because they were both dark. I know that that's so ignorant now, and I don't think in that way anymore, but I think that some people do. And that's really how they see things. As if a black person is just invisible, blending in with the background, too dark.

Then, Maralyn realized that this point of view could exist in beauty. She thought, her eyes in a daze at somewhere on her desk:

But, real, important work needs to be done before we can observe beauty in such ways. People need to be seen first. This isn't even my business, though, and I know Kyanna would remind me of that. But I can't help but see it her way; we got every Metro Boomin and Mike WiLL Made-It song to the top, America did, while ignoring the persistent plight of black Americans. We enjoyed, and glorified, their culture, while disregarding their daily suffering. Gentrified, I keep saying it,

Looking up finally, she noticed that several Triat kids had joined them. The high schoolers just chuckled at their presence, staring at the heated talkers with amused and concerned eyes like bulbs.

"We'll get all this figured out," she noticed Kyanna say. And she realized that she loved these kids, their energy was the stars and pine trees, dark-green and yellow, their conversation felt like warm fries from the carnival and genuine laughter. Naivety; acting like each other's family, taking care in that way. Of course she wanted to be a part of the sweet web, or at least have its blessing. But she still judged these friends of hers, in the way that they carried themselves, their word choices, their political statements. Like she did with other friends, yet with a veil, consistently trying to make them taken more seriously by the important people (who were mainly white) at Opifer. Nobody had asked her to save or even protect anyone, but this was her natural goal. Perhaps it had to do with her music passion. And maybe the students, "we the people," were the most important after all.

Remembering when he saw a racist note in the bathroom as a middle schooler, Sid quietly thought while sitting. The lower-class or poor Opifer kids, much of Middleton really, was in mind. Nothing had happened to spur the thoughts, but they were emotional and directed at someone.

Just because they aren't bourgeoisie doesn't make them or their predicament better. They still have white skin and features, privileges, and have to account for their actions. They don't have to be social activists, no one does at the end of the day, but they need to stay in reality. That secure, safe reality–no risk from institutions or on the streets. They won't be called a dirty nigger, or be judged as a thug or terrorizing person, ever. They call Arabs terrorists but never forget to see black people as inherently violent and dangerous. It's just fuck your privilege; it's not fair,

As if thinking back to him, Tender thought: I see how Hortz and Millington and Mr. Ryedigger look at their students–they don't see them like dirt. They see them as kind and are kind back. They're not looked at with suspicious eyes; they're normal to them. They don't have to be looked over, watched constantly from behind and above and around. There are no real conversations these days, no real people.

The discussion that day ended quickly, and so did the day. The members had headed home with Father, Eminem, or Public Enemy playing through their headphones.

“Dying” Together

“Listen, it’s about remembering who you are, and connecting with the essence inside,”

An upward emphasis is on that last word.

“But how can I connect with something which I don’t know is truly there?” She goes on, “Like, I’ve disassociated so much recently that it feels like there’s nothing inside, there even is no “self!”

It might be expected that the voice returns with a simple “nonsense,” but the path of wisdom is never this succinct. At least where it concerns *human* words, at least where it didn’t lead to broad conclusions.

Suddenly realizing that she is staring at her hand, she misses holding hands with Katrina. Although it was nearly years ago. An image of ice cold cubes, like the ones which had filled K’s glass when she was at her house for the first time, floats in her mind. Immediately after her moment with this self and Her Thought, she flails her hand around and sets it somewhere else. The adjustment is her response to electricity, partly magnetism, the warm cold, things which she has not psychologically processed yet.

“Come on, stay with me, Maralyn.”

But Maralyn only hears up to her name in that. There is more. Her fantasy is a parallel to reality. Forever existing, forever stretching forever. Or so it seems. And so it is; and so it goes. It goes.

“What?!” she exclaims.

Except it isn’t really a question.

“Yes, I’m here,”

She then rolls her eyes.

“I’ll be here; I’ll fucking be here, I’m here,”

Dwing.

Chapter 17

Thoughtful Spacing in Nowhere

A very bright light glowed from every square of the floor. Hence each white tile blended into the other. Eyesight was focused, movements directed; the embodiment of "on your mark, get set, go!"

Josiah's curving ankles danced, traversing the little corners of the territory which he claimed.

at something around. A dominant social force breathed, recognizing an epicenter begging to be gasped at and grasped. It was a centerpiece in the room without borders. But, this space was not necessarily endless. It had character. Its vitality was contained within particular boundaries. And existence in it was without regard for different places, other spaces, foreignality.

A moment of pause was reached for some. Maralyn saw, in her mindfield, pastel-based designs with their faint edges. They would float around, puzzle pieces and squares, and fling, fly. The shapes would donate themselves, go back to themselves again, passing the young girl by.

"There's no meaning," Josiah then said, quietly. Without much inflection or emotion.

A few kids watched him, looking for voice cracks. His eyes seemed crazy and almost mad to them. His lifetone reminded many of the decrepit group at home from Tim Burton's *Charlie and the Chocolate Factory.*

"Meaning is everything here,"

Afterwards, he swiftly turned his entire body and commenced a terrifying bounce. The boy was jumping up and down, almost in a full shake after a single moment. But they could discern his incredible amount of deep joy.

Those who had observed him now listened to his spirit. In his example, but pursuing their unique urge, many flipped around to twist and shift their bodies this way and that.

Rosie walked a rectangular box that led from the central point to the forming stage. The shape did not end concretely, though, the edges were blurred. When they saw her. Her name, to the kids, brought to mind the face of a flower. Round, magenta, petals in groups of four, an almost comical structure affixed to futile green lines.

Spoken words ended as randomly as they began, here. Sentences were dead, always. Sentiments were unborn, but some were growing beings.

A Question Which Nobody Thought to Ask

The rectangular, box-like figure revealed itself, in a slow dissolve. The stage with panels of brown wood and a glassy, grey surface planted. A darkening glow surrounded these intruders, but they were being sent love by those present still.

They continued to dance for a few moments forward; everybody was choosing to ignore the latest structure. Never tiring, never letting up

While facing downwards, a stern look of meditative concentration engraved into her, Marilyn sent out a thought to every direction: Somebody get up there.

"Now get up, get up, let's go!"

Her face clean of acne scars and wrinkles was like the sun under the lights.

The stage was almost done assembling, coating itself in fresh, safe concrete. Some kids even thought to jump on it, as pieces were being put together, invisible hands exhausting.

The dream was over. Maralyn was still sleeping. She reached the peak of her calm. Her senses told her to ignore everything else. As a person, when she began to focus, there was great light inside and near her.

There just wasn't enough room for an ego.

The labels and calls of other people… "they're like white noise." These are fragments that float above the black penmarks and which are more truthful and real to her.

I can see your lack of attention, that's actually a call to attention. Actually/already.

But her brain ruined the more she analyzed and recorded the twists and shifts inside of reality.

"Give up." a loud, coarse voice interrupted. A clear, flaming command.

Then, realized the statement: I'm doing this because I want to. Autonomy, my choice, pain.

"We are in France now,"

Portions of lavender colored walls, darkened by twilight. Her brain was sending messages to her, this simply among them.

"What?" she would later ask her brain during fully cognizant.

But anyways, sleeping on sateen pillow cases and celebrating your birthday… Plane ride to France,

Memes Catalyze Self-Personalization

An idea is born–transmits across the surface and through brains like leaves–absorbed so it is invisible. Forever in debt to your new complaint. Erase me. Delete me. Can you feel the Past, whatever they think of as our city's history? Our place?!

"Can you feel it now, Maralyn? Can you hear it all from here?"

Dipping the blackberries in cottage cheese, finally real food, then landing scoops into the mouth. The cheeks are slightly dry; so does the hungry body feel. Basketball courts. Bouncing balls on it. Let it in. "Let it happen." Let it begin; you are a mature girl. No, not you. The other one.

Stanza three. There's a dog sleeping on the brown couch; does he realize he's being glared at? Learning the history of American slavery in fifth grade, scanning the books for provocative drawings of black lines being lined up in large boats. This is supposed to represent "the transportation of black slaves to the West." To the West. To the West.

To the West.

Who. Now Just perfectly vague. Choke me to death. Asphyxiate.

Woo. Deathing. Rhyming.

What did you do? To me,

Fucking bitch.

Grandiosity. A delusion.

So Josiah's observations about his close friends began.

But I would never act on my hatred, I'm not that psycho. I'm not one. Duh. Maybe, I'd commit suicide–if that meant sparing everyone else. No, but that's not what I mean.

He realized his paranoia.

I mean like, if I live on like this, I won't contribute to good and positive things, so it'd be better if I was dead,

In that case. Yeah.

And then he felt like listening to Nirvana. Yet, his inner figures stopped him.

"That would be weird," they said. "That would be lame."

So what the fuck should I listen to? he asked them.

Josiah mindlessly took out his phone from his front pocket.

I'm going to listen to some Ringo Deathstarr.

pepe

°Feeln good, listening to new ska and exploring genres° Henry had randomly Tweeted the evening before today.

Josiah had replied with, °bro. same, i feel u. ive been listening to so much radiohead lately°

That's not anything like ska but I'll accept it, Henry had thought.

°Word°

Then they had texted each other.

°What's up dude° Henry had responded to Jay's initiation.

Nothing much, just thinking about you, he had wanted to say.

°just chilling here, minding my own business° °trying to listen to weird music°

°Isn't your dad like a really talented pianist? That's so cool°

°oh, haha° °yes he is, thank you ill tell him°

°but he wants me to be exactly like that, which is hard to say the least°

°Oh lol I feel you, my mom was like that about being a businessperson° And a few moments later, °But i just have to focus on music°

Josiah had felt comfortable with their relatability.

°oh btw° °your recent instagram selfie is cute.°

°just thought i should put that out there°

And with that, Josiah had locked his phone and tossed it onto the bed. Jesus christ I just said that, he thought.

°Lol, thank you bro° Henry replied back. °Gotta get da looks up for the girlz and all them .°

°oh, yes. i completely feel you dude° sent Josiah. But, he really hadn't.

Students like Trevor and Henry, they couldn't get on par with upper-rank Projects, even if they worked on them for years. They could dedicate the most part of evenings for months on end to fashioning a beautiful video, but it would not change their grade point legacy, research papers, or looks. If they aced their papers, there would be bias against them on Video Day or in class. These were the kids who "got Cs and Bs." It was the way they were to institution and it was immobile. Kids' positions were a common, albeit subliminal, understanding.

Trevor looked up to, rather than next to, people like Ryan and his friends. Even though he was the same age or older. The half-Filipino Leila and her friends, usually including the blonde Ryan when he wasn't doing a leadership takeover of another "upper-class" group, were the Honors Squad. Maralyn and her friends called them this because they took every Honors class possible, together, including ones available at Sigma only (World History, Computer Science, Advanced Geography, Chinese). They would hop in the main elevator and walk their unbelonging selves up to 15 minutes to class.

It was deeply apparent that most of their teachers respected them. And they pushed them as models or examples. It was just that socially aware and experienced kids had a problem with it. Maralyn, Josiah too, felt that the balance of opportunity and kindness was out of whack, disadvantageous for even most students.

Maralyn, Rosie, Henry (and more, really) ridiculed them for obsessively sticking together: nearly identical schedules every semester, religiously collaborating on assignments and exams since elementary school, ignoring students who were not on the same level or did not respect theirs. It was clear to Rosie that the main thing which held them together was their tradition; this perfect history of excellence and purity, not authentic synergy. Their connection was religious, without a God. Their pursuit of material success was a self-fulfilling obsession. At a certain point, around sophomore year, a few members began to branch off when secular hours were over; one of them even tried weed. But they never broke and always came back.

A black one, a half-Asian one, a Jewish one, and two white ones–Maralyn would think–wow! What perfect diversity! And fantastic parents who show up to everything and take them places, similar-minded siblings, constant stability, cupcake shops with friends on the weekend. No wonder they do well on everything! Every single thing,

With these frameworks at the top birthed, other groups got around, well, in the ways that they did. At first (from first to ninth grade), Henry, Jordan, Brett, and formerly Trevor, were conniving, disorderly kids–generally feared or avoided by teachers during the beginning of a school year. They would never directly show this to them, the boys' rowdy charisma helped there, but would subtly twist their hopes from the inside out.

To persist. Today.

"Hey, Mr. Willis!" Henry shouted after his new posse bumped into him in the hallway. He was lowkey trying to impress them. The man's unsettled face made things even more amusing for the boys.

"Hi there," the teacher hesitated. After silence, he asked, "Henry. Yes?"

"Knock, knock,"

He had to think about that one for a second.

"Who's there?"

He then subtly wished for the group to somehow evaporate, or get slapped in the faces by a bitter Mrs. Millington.

"Your refrigerator," he replied.

"Your refrigerator who?"

Like he didn't even realize what he himself was doing, Henry quickly turned around and zoomed down the hallway.

Mr. Willis was stuck with a perfectly blank face in the boy's direction. His arms subtly dangled at his sides, his core somewhat deflated.

The group's crackling laughter boomed when they saw his reaction. Their voices were as if through an amp, and contagious to even people in the hallway whom they didn't know. Walking there with Trevor, Katrina started giggling with them, and she didn't even know what the joke was. Her laughter shone everybody's day, including Mr. Willis'–never to be mentioned by him.

When Could There Ever Be Evil In Blankness?

The boy we study sits watching.

As we come closer, our eyes zoom in from behind his little head to the screen. It is large now. We see inside.

"Maralyn, Maralyn, Maralyn,"

What? she began to think. Bothered.

In a tone more serious: "Don't you know you can't do that?"

Pause. Silent.

"They won't let you,"

There was a crack of innocence, probably born of ignorance, in Ms. Genevieve's voice.

The screen fizzles in white noise for one second. And so there was a steady and lengthy rupture down the teenager's middle. Her long brown hair hid it away. Her perfectly oval eyes stored the exhibition of a normalcy which was no secret. There was no secret at all.

Name

The room's blue walls were comforting, and little bumps in the paint made like glitter as late sun rays hit them. A flock of birds, that knew each other she guessed, squawked from a nearby tree. It was annoying.

It had been an extremely hectic day–taking a Project
software vocabulary exam, taking care of Josiah crying about a boy and his homophobic parents, drawing posters for Project: Creative Day–so respite was hers.

Maralyn let the spider on her floor be as she sighed, sprawled on her bed. The post-cyber trance let in whatever thoughts that may have come.

Wow… A lot happened today, she thought.

Gee golly, she literally said in her head, why does Katrina piss me off so much,

She swallowed uncomfortably.

No, it's not Katrina that aggravates me, makes me lose self-control (whether it's really her fault or not). It's people like Genevieve and Millington with their actions that ignore me, and push down other kids' goals. It kills the motivation, whatever of it that we have left.

She came to her final realization of the night: this, everything that the current week offered, was everything. A typical slice of time could just be composed of spending the day at school and savoring every bit of freedom. Or it could look like chilling on the weekend.

Maralyn remembered what Jesse had told her in private the other day, that her boyfriend Henry lowkey made her feel uneasy at times. And she had never felt genuine, true affection for a boy before. And although she knew deep down that whatever orientation was okay, she didn't know that it was *okay*. It was a type of guilt expressed along with anxiety, the first born of pure fear. It was not easy for anyone, in any setting in any area in the world in any time period, to be non-heterosexual. "I understand," Maralyn had told her.

What was the confirmation that she really did? What separated Maralyn from her friend? The most important question revolved around whether or not the teenagers should feel so divided about their emotions in the first place.

The intentions. Calculated in this detachment, their intentions would end up even more mature. So, really, it was not a bad thing. Were there evil omens in this blank objectivity?

She envisioned the bookish hallways between Middleton and Sigma and resonated with a warm peace stored inside the memory. She saw Katrina's hateful eyes, again. Except that maybe it was Maralyn's personal filters which made them so, and she knew better than to judge an ambiguous situation using assumptive lenses. Did she? Anyways, Rosie's merry smile came into view and was a good thing to recount. Then a few minutes went by. Quickly shutting "The Alchemist" because she couldn't concentrate, she took her beanie off and went to sleep mentally planning out her Project.

"They say they gon' kill me
What you waiting for, bitch?"
–Thirteen13 - Death To All Posers

There was no flow here. Only psychopathy, chaos, dark, blood, madness, shame, vice. No connections. Bad memories. Real, assured affirmation of the ugly ideas–"yes" to the self-destructive thoughts. There were weird shapes, weird shapes of the human body, animals, circles and triangles and squares; suicide of philosophy and the person who had created it. Bright black background; flowers with neon petals and no stems or sepals. Appearing, spinning lightly. Flashes of white areas and stripes, but their duration lasted the blink of an eye.

Big, deep, dark smile.

Indeed, Katrina formulated, indeed. Making art will always be better than homework, motherfuck every teacher. And y'all know what else? How we dress when we leave the house is like an inevitable statement, about who you are and who you're gonna attract. So I'm saying goodbye to that flex shit and wearing all white rags from now on, dish cloths and towels.

Fuck it.

Sapphism

Her ego would, silently, shut off all of her light(s). One by one, row by row.

It took away, vacuumed and stole and stored away or discarded, her human existence vocabulary. It would steal it, steal it more, if she was not brutishly careful about her actions and experiences.

Who do you choose to be around? voiced a thousand, million miles away from a center in the Universe. It was a grand, important question.

Cry Baby

"Haha! Yeah, I'm turning 17 in two months," Katrina loudly voiced to the friend group in front of her.

Nobody but her and the group "leader," Nick, knew that there was secret between them. It was about a boy and other futile topics.

Josiah changed the song to "dial flower" by drew the architect, featuring drip-133.

"Nice," Nick lowly responded, to him.

This inspired the friend to sensually, calmly grin at Katrina.

"You're so cool," Nick told Katrina a moment later.

Maralyn felt young when Katrina had told them that. She was turning 18 this month and nobody besides her mother had mentioned anything about it thus far. She felt that this group, half from Sigma half from a school a few miles away, had secret interests in mind–a putting above of the incongruous personality which was the most normal, normal like them. And that description fit Katrina.

I just need some support, she thought. Or maybe I'm overthinking things. Overthinking everything,

The entire group released a burst of laughter, an eruption really, but Maralyn missed why.

Katrina remained blushing, and slightly confused, about her boy–although ex-lovers were present which made things awkward, but hers was a happy, silly freedom. Maralyn remained salty to her because of the topic. That night, she took it upon herself to make sure nobody invited her to Jesse's upcoming Project work session, especially since Katrina never seemed to show gratitude for getting homework help for free.

Basely, the girl felt erased–whether she realized any of her actions or not.

Chapter 18

He burped while dragging his sore feet up to the floor C. Josiah had made three rounds, counting this, of carrying Opifer gardening materials outside.

"Josiah, do you think you could help me with something?" Ms. Hortz asked as she lifted her tired back up. There were four or five more boxes to go.

His face reacted in frankness. Not completely annoyance. His lips were fresh and red with recent emotion, and they leaned forward before he responded.

"Yeah, I think I could help you,"

The bottoms of his black and white Chuck Taylors were coated in dried mud. They had been transferring storage from her room to one of the school vans. The paperwork, books, and posters would sit in her basement for a little while before August came around. There was a slight solemnity in the dark brown benches nearby, as well as in the enfant wind that encircled them now. They both took turns sighing. It was nearing five pm, and lots of work had gotten done today. An intensive cycle of exams was occurring–he avoided the crossfires, rather diving into extracurricular and Project work.

Ms. Hortz was a young woman, with a boyfriend whom many of the students knew about, but acted oddly warm to her male students. She had a strange, yet naturally close, bond with Josiah.

When she first met him earlier in the year, she assumed that his affection was rooted in sexual attraction. But she tried to stifle all of these thoughts. With ulterior meaning, though: the ideas themselves were inappropriate, but nothing or no one could ever change real feelings. She had always been insecure about her harsh, messy voice, which sounded like salty shouting out even while speaking quietly. Her accent was sassy and dumb-seeming. She liked her students making her more confident. The teacher had no idea of course that Josiah was gay.

Summon Me Again

Why do they keep on using me? Katrina thought.

Don't use me like an enzyme, Maralyn thought, use me to get something difficult done and then disregard me forever. Keep me in good condition, don't abandon me. You know I can't deal with the salt or heat.

She set her school things aside and ruminated on the choice of mind-numbing activities she could partake in this weekend.

Why would you be doing it if your heart's not in it?

Big large ideas. It's not about the memes, even when it is, Maralyn wrote down. I can be an asshole, I know, and so can the whole Internet. We regress and regress and ingest "mechanical" chemicals, really just updated versions of our parents' vices. And that and the Internet help to slow us and our thoughts down.

We begin to not make sense. We don't focus on the things that "matter", like school and family and being a good citizen. But, every student hates school - maybe angst is forever. I'm just scribbling at this point. I know less people smoke today, but no one has ever experienced the Internet and what it can do.

Why would you hail yourself as a Senior if you can't even set a positive example?

Katrina grimaced reacting at the contents of her phone and everything around her. A brown candle was burning on her desk; it rested alongside a glass of lime water and outsplayed arms.

Leaning into the device, she had spent forty five minutes observing an argument inside her "Trevor and Henry group chat," so called because they were the primary people who it was about.

They were, it seemed, fighting about credibility and honesty–a question of who would be the designated-driver this Saturday. It incited an argument about the members' varying levels of drug tolerance, and Henry's so-called feigned ability to drive after having drunk a few hours before.

°You can't even walk steady or talk to people when you've just drank a little. how the fuck do you expect to drive? i wouldn't let you drive me.° so Trevor's diatribical texts came out.

She felt erased in the conversation. It wasn't new, but it seemed like when important topics came up, suddenly her several experiences did not apply anymore and they would take over control. Even with her knowledge of designated-driving, low tolerance, and both Henry and Trevor.

They were genuinely heated, so maybe it was a good thing that she wasn't getting involved. Maybe something was protecting her from that. She did not know about "someone," though.

Brown People . People With Dark Features

"She loves to lay, I'm all to blame
I learned the hard way"
–Love To Lay - The Weeknd

The stairway she sat on scanning was dark grey on top, concrete on bottom interpolated yellow strips. She couldn't believe such could be made of anything more than white forms outlined in grey and contrasted by all the blacks.

Katrina was in her grey Air Force 1s with shiny grey material and rainbow-showered soles. The guilt that overtook her almost every night subsided a little. It was like gentle raindrops which flew from right to left at a slant, which moved so fast that they seemed like webs in the air. Tonight in her mindscape was true clarity–she held onto it, her knuckles had no intention on loosening their grip.

Thanks for doing you. And thanks for always placing the blame on me.

Chapter 19

The Price We Pay for Knowledge is Through Paypal

°im suffering, and idk if anybody knows or cares°

Josiah was on the brink of hitting Send on the Tweet, it was perfectly transcribed from his mind, but there was a block.

He had been struggling, depressive anxiety shaking up toe to head in the days through nights. But who wanted to know or care about that? Plenty of irrational and fearful ideas, stories ran through his head all week.

What he actually Tweeted was, °keep holding on - slum village°

He didn't even have enough energy to type the lyric which made him Tweet it: "See that's Satan making my heart cold as a breeze, 'till it's frozen."

The kids lived in a world which had ultra/mega-accessible television, videos, live horror stories, yellowed pies with their set oil, music, performances, humor, cultural events, and the nightly news–either in roundtable discussions or article titles. As the boy Josiah stared up at their ceiling while his parents participated in these things, he thought: these are the things that give me depression. I'm disgusted, this gives me disgust,

He knew–he realized after having a few good conversations with the school therapist–that he should improve his condition via healthy hobbies and consumption, yet he felt stuck. Stuck in his inability to turn his blindness into cultural, ethical, moral reality. And some kids were lost further. He didn't know or see it, but the stuckness was there, not in his capabilities as a functioning young human being. The kids he tutored and kids Elias' age were inundated in this transformed lifestyle, more global, just as fast, since young, young ages. So, in a way, he felt lucky, but also really no, not at all. I don't know, he'd think, nothing makes me feel better; none of this does.

Jay joined his family again, mentally; he couldn't forget about or escape from the taste of their microwaveable chicken alfredo plates, from hours earlier, or even the smell of them on his face. He was so sad; stuck, sad, strunk–forever, or something like that.

And he just wanted it to be over. He wanted it all to be over. Josiah sighed with the realization that he had wasted too many hours of his life, many of them probably very precious, sulking inwardly instead of living. He felt that he had wasted potential; something inside or outside of him pulled joy from the tear it had made. And evidently, it did not stop pulling. He always heard about "living life to the fullest," especially on the Internet, but it was so hard to when his parents or friends told him different stories. Stories about being fucked up, not being inspired, not repenting, losing everyday in life, and watching successful people from afar.

Who is going to be the change? he wondered. Probably not me.

The girl Maralyn sat on her crumby warm bed, laughing at videos of a nature YouTuber sting himself with various brutal wasps and ants.

Beds are usually warm (or hot), but sitting here that night, it was cold.

Separately. Equally.

“Sometimes girls can get us through hard times. The usual turmoil of human lives, but all people are special.” Trevor wrote in his notebook.

He had set his book report aside, deciding to just go with the flow of the cooling night.

“What I remember about it is that she always really wanted to impress me,” Katrina softly says, to the camera. She is comfortable talking now, but would rather be submitting texts to the system.

Katrina appreciates conversation of all kinds and via all media, but using her thumbs to confidently sculpt ideas was so simple and smooth.

After she takes out her phone, she types into their ProjectPortals messages, °she always made sure that i spoke to her if she was dressed up nice that day, or something° °like a cute dress or something!°

°Is that true?° he will ask Maralyn later, to which she’ll respond, °No. Well I mean, it wasnt intentional°

The kid recalls all the video and text entries Katrina had made complaining about it.

°Oh, I thought that really bothered you?°

°lol it was annoying then, but once she stopped i just felt sorta lonely and empty at times°

Oh, he thinks.

°it was just, nice… it was cute, but our friendship wasnt that cute, or close. so° She edited that one a few times over first.

°Oh i see°

°one time, she came in in this really cute green and orange flannel, that was like, from a famous streetwear brand or something, and her hair was in two braids and ripped jeans. she looked lovely back then, she was in general°

°i miss that part of her°

While he digests her messages for a minute, he realizes that other guys probably revel at the idea of Maralyn and Katrina officially hooking up, but he is personally above it–better than that and them.

°I understand° he replies in time for her to not disappear completely.

Nervously sitting on the loveseat in her room, she reflects on all the words and swallows.

°yeah, thanks I'm glad°

She realizes that this probably sounded condescending, to either him or Maralyn, so she follows up with: °i honestly remember those days like it was yesterday°

°damnn° he quickly responds.

He doesn't want to hear anymore about this.

Bwing!

Deathblown Eyes

Maralyn and Jay met at their lot. They went deeper inside, to one of the clearings inside of the surrounding forest. His demeanor seemed like he had something to say, possibly even controversial, a lot on his mind. When they settled in, he paced around and she stayed leaning back on a rusty silver bar.

"What's up?" His voice crackled, like a fire, out of apparent fatigue and distress. "What's good, Maralyn,"

"What's good," she responded uppily yet more tiredly. Her voice cracked from all the smoking.

"My birthday is soon," Josiah said wearily. "17, babyy,"

"Yaaay," she flatly responded. She then searched her back pockets for something.

"What are we gonna do?"

Maralyn felt her phone buzz onto her butt, finally dragging it out.

While checking it, she responded, "Well, I don't know. I do know that we are going to finish our video because the Projects are coming up! You know,"

To Josiah, the Project deadline had the same urgency for her as checking her apps for updates.

"So, why don't you finish it?" he told her, with sour eyebrows. It was still indifferent. "You have all my parts, I did all the singing and modeled in the video."

She stopped moving and talking, paused. The girl looked around, feeling the cold bar against her back, scanning for the dying sun behind their clouds. She scratched her thigh with the other heel, then let at least 20 seconds drift by. Josiah had planted his feet into the ground.

After clearing his throat, "Well?"

Maralyn? Oh. Hello? he thought cynically.

"Oh yeah, hey, sorry. Listen, Josiah…" she replied. "It's that it's been on my mind a lot, you know how it is, and there are many reasons for me wanting to succeed...in it, and like stuff in the Project Portal has been bothering me too. So there's a lot going on,"

She said the last parts almost secretively.

"Oh yeah? What do you mean by that, though?"

Okay then there it is, the reasons she doesn't care about her friend's depression or birthday coming up, he thought.

The green of the trees was more accentuated to him now, while she unknowingly wished that their spot would become bluer and blacker out.

"I don't know; like, Katrina, and stuff. And that kid who's been weird on it, again sorta,"

He furrowed his brows deeply. "What do you mean? he asked almost incredulously. "I know that kid, the regular dude, and he's been getting really close to Katrina and kids from Middleton."

He felt ridiculous saying Katrina's name in ideas like those, almost feeling bad for her.

"But he's always doing something weird. What do you mean with Katrina?"

Maralyn was absolutely dumbfounded. Katrina and her had never even formally acknowledged the communications together. What was she telling Josiah, and why not her? They had been using the Portals to basically "bond" for months now; what did the little Josiah know about their world?

"I didn't even know you knew about all that," she responded. "That's kinda weird. All I was trying to talk about was the videos. Nevermind,"

"Videos." She was embarrassed about the Iraqi-American influences in her accent; It sounded like vee-dee-ohs. Even though Josiah had never brought it up or commented on it. But she taught herself one day that human dialogue is based on a fragile cesspool of ideas, often lending itself of pure irrationality and hatred.

He shot back, "Well, how is it weird when you're apparently on there all the time? And like not doing anything else,"

Maralyn was offended, but she didn't want to talk about it. "No, I mean, I don't really care–do what you want, I just am so confused."

She suddenly noticed something disturbing, which she had no idea how to respond to. Her first instinct was ranting about it on Twitter later, or texting Heather about it, because it was rude. But for now, it was a paralyzing fear. Josiah's eyes seemed like canvases of dried black paint, devoid of shine or connection and their usual rainbows.

"Hello?" she nervously mustered out.

You didn't see the signs, he thought, you didn't notice,

His gaze was focused to the top of his friend's head, not particularly looking there. A long eight seconds went by. Maralyn realized that she wanted Starbucks.

"How are you fucking confused," he laughed. "We all go to the same school. We all have emails and access to whatever online shit is going on right now, even at school. I talk to that kid, and Katrina, all the time,"

"You *talk* to him?"

"Well, no, I don't fucking talk to him but I do think I know him from the stuff he shares and watches. I actually have a lot in common with some of it. And maybe he's not even a boy, maybe he's making a social media profile with it or something,"

They both felt heavy with the particular knowledge, almost guilty about it, that this person was still a complete stranger to everybody. He could have been a pedophile for all they knew, and it was important not to become too close to him. But, out of all people, Maralyn cared the least.

"Okay, fair," she responded. "I guess,"

"So yeah, stop being salty about it and thinking about the Project due date all the time and realize that your friends are just trying to be happy. Like, care about my birthday, or something." And he huffed.

"Jeez," she told him. She said it again in her head.

"Well, just good luck to us both getting good grades on it, and happy early birthday to you. Sorry."

Although it was half-assed, Josiah was content with that. For now.

He left the forest that day upset that his best friend seemed to barely give a shit anymore. About him, about anything real and important.

This is fucking why I don't have social media–he happily told himself, as they marched to his aging car.

Chapter 20

"Lick my wounds with honey,
Save me for the vultures
I'm fallin' in the void,
I don't know what I discover"
–Dom of Brockhampton - TRIP

In the midst of Maralyn finalizing angles and filters for their video, her and her laptop in the nicer Opifer library, on Floor A. Her hands sifted through the volumes and papers that she had placed in front of her. A yellow and black designed copy of *Mrs. Dalloway* appeared.

The words "Virginia Woolf" seemed to speak out loud, to have a voice. And they did.

"So, you think you can be like me?" the voice interjected at the girl, from a quaint woman's animated face there. "You want to try to be me or something?"

Maralyn's spine froze.

"Huh? Hmm?" the legendary writer interjected. "Speak!"

"I'm scared." Maralyn mumbled.

"Is that what you would like? Let us all know!"

For the first time in Maralyn's life, she felt scared of what she absolutely did not know. The historic woman simply gazed back at her. A shiver, the cerebrovascular system; truth realized in yummy, trippy fragments–all of this could in no way be finite, but her mind had limitations. Overpowering, her robotic vocals which were strong enough to be a part of earth's bassline itself, finally finding peace in the noise. In the dark, when a production's cover art stabbed at her eyes, that's when Maralyn appreciated hard work the most. Because it was hard; the scaly ribcage or crying bird informed her heart of a human magic that was caring. A genuine human dance; creator and listener together daring.

This may not be the *point*, she thought, of life. But these works lead people on a type of road that ends somewhere, somewhere different, and they've personally guided me on my way out of the darkness. So thanks for that.

As cliché as things could be. As disruptive a poet could be the within the confines/rules/laws of a particular genre.

She then realized, as Woolf's breath faded away: as long as she as an individual paid respects to the those responsible for art, she could sleep, study, and rage in peace.

Damn. she was hot, Maralyn thought as she flopped a new book atop *Mrs. Dalloway.*

And then she noticed something peculiar: the following quote on a book's half ripped out page:

"This is it, the darkest hour.
Isn't it depressing how our
Minds create an atmosphere
That won't happen here,
Unless we make some new demands
To grasp the future in our hands."

Maralyn pushed the top of the page back inside, skimming the band Agent Orange's biography. The hardcover was *The History of Punk Rock Music From Its Inception to 2006*, compiled and edited by a large music foundation. Maralyn then lifted it up and down to feel its heftiness. She then opened it to a random page.

Chris Cornell, with the camera at his kneeling knees and a microphone nearly inside his gaping mouth, seemed to be screaming lyrics. From the vantage point of the stage floor, the sweaty definition of his chest and dark hair were highlighted. Pink and red strobe lights abounded. A few pages before the Soundgarden and Audioslave spread contained a press photo of 2002 Dave Grohl beaming, attending some sort of celebrity event.

Maralyn smiled back and slammed the book shut. She would leave in 30 minutes, or as soon as her mom was ready to pick her up.

She would do nothing when she got home and nothing the next day, even while at school.

Toy Plane

Later on, that same week. Maralyn, in her dad's car, drove swiftly forward.

Alone on this dirt road. A faint yellow aura emitted by the headlights revealed her path. It did not tell the way, though. So she used the Google Maps application.

Normally, the girl would feel uncomfortably lost under the brooding evergreen in these areas. But with one hand on the wheel and the other on her rose golden phone, it was the boys and girls who did it tonight. Her ones. She figured that, she was lost because they made her so.

And this disintegration was her revenge.

She would not, almost could not, look away from the street. She shakily had the phone near her face, rather than looking at it during stop signs.

Soon would be the last turn, and then Katrina's house to her left. She suddenly tossed the iPhone into a cupholder, without a thought. And the radio was put zero a few moments after she left her house.

Slowing down for her last few minutes alone, Maralyn gave in and looked about the car's interior. Its hefty grey wheel seemed to bulge out at her, with a sinister technological quality. She had no conception of evil at this point in life, only the fact of the machinery under her sensitive touch. And now the little icons which told lifesaving information, such as speed and time, but also the radio station and song title. These were all glaring back at her, just as suspiciously as her. The wheels screeched.

A perception of great injustice felt up the girl through her veins, starting at the gut. Maralyn went 15 mph.

Katrina's home was a long ways down this road. The only sounds there were the blowing of the tired engine and old tires crunching over differently sized rocks. Her phone buzzed, possibly, and a popular R&B song strode its name across the tiny screen. But she did not register this. Houses nearby were awake, as their open curtains and children playing outdoors revealed. And then there was, still, the vehicle.

Mostly every bit of human awareness inside focused on what was in front, on the robust, linear path. After another minute, the girl's eyes began to strain to see. Her vision became encased inside of a rectangular filter of weak white. The future of her evening would be ensured by its uncertain fogginess. This paranoid aesthetic threatened to spoil a normal, stable mental state for the entire night out with friends. In this lack of focus, with its myopic taste for non-life, Maralyn really did not know anything.

The moral lessons she had learned before, she had to let go of, her mind forgetting them one by one. Experiences into a positive, gentle recovery lost her. They could not offer much solace in this slow, dangerous moment, anyways. They meant nothing because they simply were not real. Anymore.

Innocent ruminations about the former world, the one shattered, presented themselves to her. She remembered her mom now, with little emotion but in high definition:

"It will all go away. Don't think about everything too much! Take it easy and things will be okay with time,"

Her faded white was getting closer, becoming more intimate. The reality filter was like a haunted and long-forgotten item from a desolate antique shop. Nobody wanted anything to do with it. Buyers desired to escape those halls, with their crackling archways and dusty floors. Or, the mental cage was like a film forbidden in forty-five countries. Its 3,000 leftover DVD copies would have been in tight handling by a most obsessive, probably perverted, collector. Form regardless, the teenager's creation was a gift of nature that smelled of burning hair.

And a voice inside her mind quickly shot back at her mother:

"That…does not exist! No. Not right. This is everything, and it is not okay, I am not okay. It won't go away. I'm not thinking right now, Mom,"

With that, the hope that held Maralyn up in her failed her. The car felt as if it drifted through atmospheres as it missed Katrina's house. She opened her window after reaching a barren dead-end. There, were decayed brown leaves, muddy soda bottles, and a decades-old soccer ball.

The breeze was extremely brisk. It felt like pure numbing of the skin. A lone streetlamp, which glowed an intense yellow atop its skinny green pole, was plunked next to a likely defunct drinking fountain. Maralyn hurriedly observed these details, all foreign–not out of curiosity, but survival. Her animal instincts wanted her to remain safe, despite what the rest of her mind was putting her through. Still the girl realized none of this. If she had been in a calmer state, maybe she would have appreciated the spot and asked Katrina to explore it together. Her line of sight, then, never truly came back to the wheel, or the radio, or the time, or her phone. It never came back to inside the car, where her physical and experience were themselves.

Her grainy, yet shiny and glaring, cream film did not let up. The feeling, the perception, and the spirit of it overpowered her. Maralyn found herself forming one coherent thought:

I just wanted to hang out with my friends,

And that was the thought which broke her, like an earthquake smashing land in half. Evil did too fill in the empty cracks. Her dry hands, now without much blood, squeezed the steering wheel.

Maralyn entered a zone of concentration, enveloping her body. In the few short pauses during the black hole journey, which did not allow time for deep breathing, she hyperventilated–while weeping.

"Crying for nothing. No…without a cause," she told herself with gritted teeth. "Meaningless, everything is."

The seat shook as she rocked back and forth. The back of her head slammed into the headrest a few times. Twice, she jabbed her forehead against the top of the wheel. Accidentally or purposefully. The machine and its oppressiveness.

Maralyn could not undo the high quality of her current sensitivity. It would just dissolve into itself, she would forget about every word. Something, a camera's light inside of her brain, turned on–like it turned itself on. Her self was still adamant on being oil to water, but her spirit very slowly moved her otherwise. As she aggressively kicked her knees up and down onto the plastic circle above, the material nature of her surrounds began to exist again. There was suddenly color in the world; her vision was clearing. This brought a tiny bit of relief. And her neck had enough power to look around again, her body enough for strength as well.

Her phone started ringing as soon as she picked it up to nonsensically check Instagram. The call washed away the odd shame that she normally felt after panic attacks. It was time to go. They'd leave the house, which was 40 feet away, for town later and she was their ride.

"Hello?"

"Heyyy," Rosie asked in an expectant, sing-songy voice. "Where you at?"

"Almost there. Be there in two minutes,"

"Okay, for sure."

"See you soon,"

Tap.

Maralyn used the few made-up minutes to blow her nose, drink half a bottle of warm water, and reapply her mascara. She made sure that everything in the car was organized, no evidence of her gruesome breakdown was left behind. Before backing out of the deserted spot and into a driveway to turn around, she vocally thanked the metal garbage bin outside for its services.

Maralyn then thought about calling her mom later on. She hoped, with a little bright thing deep down under, that she would remember to do it.

It was deeply unsettling, looking to the left and catching the weird math teacher overlooking the hall. At least he wasn't genuinely creepy, like a lot of the ones before, Maralyn thought, but hey! That's a horrible thing to think.

She ignored the fatbellied man. He did that in a new spot every day.

On the top of her list today was the upcoming chemistry test; Katrina was right up next.

Thoughts of her didn't carry a burdenous weight, like an test or an adult whom kids must know how to defend themselves against. You know, like genuinely creepy teachers and pedophiles. Yet, the thoughts stuck to her at the feet, slowly bringing her down like it was molasses dripping from the knees. Always, everyday. It seemed.

But the ever-important question stood, as assertively as ever: Was her discomfort a result of Katrina, or her mental construction of Katrina? In other words, was it Maralyn's own fault, her whole life to blame, or their relationship with one another? And if both, how?

Questions. Sad?

And Maralyn was led into a harrowing cathedral. Yards of mini flowers hugged the small piece of land. There was the scent of a dusty garage sale rising from the rocks.

The pathway had a shining–gorgeous and intimidating–mosaic of yellows, light blues, and green.

The boy lit his cigarette. His thighs were cramped from the uphill stroll. He was getting older, he realized he should go to the gym more and pay attention to his thin lower body.

Maybe I'll need a cane by my 30s, he thought.

They headed in from a back door. He entered a three-digit key at the hefty door. The girl felt like she might leap with joy. Yes the walk had exhausted her, but it was like a pure summer, and the sense soon subdued.

"The walk was worth it, wasn't it," he asked.

"Yeah," she mutters in awe.

They scaled either side, a column of pews between them.

Maralyn stared up at Mary, who was staring into her, and then the rectangular outline illuminated in purple. That was the Virgin's characteristic color, the color she was often portrayed in. Maybe she did wear it often.

She reflected on the depiction. Her fragmented thoughts composed themselves on their own: the woman seemed to know what everybody individually knew. But also what nobody knew.

Exiting the establishment, the two held hands atop the dirt road nearby and were off towards the green forestry.

The event had naturally occurred. No coercion or hesitation on either side, just plain nonverbal consent. Maralyn half-grinned now. The sun painted the sky a base yellow, yet still was a white and screaming orb. If money was real, it had no currency.

Trevor sighed–depressed and broken and young.

He said after nervously swallowing. "She broke the time,"

A pause happened.

"Our time, she stole it, all of my time,"

His slicked back hair looked stupid to Maralyn now. She was sure that Josiah still cared about these topics of his, and that justified her reaction in some odd way. But not quite.

Another pause later, she realized that she missed reading books outside with her English class. Or something like that: happening in spring, under the shade of the collective happiness which a for-once unified group introduced. Especially at Opifer.

Then, here. Still?

Her eyes peered out of her anxious shadowed face, looking for a collective hero, silently speaking: this is so pointless.

"What is the point, anyways?"

Maralyn, felt the holes–the games and ladders tearing her friends apart.

Why? For What?

I could never feel deeper than this–she thought–there is no time more meaningful than this, but here we are spending it like this. Tearing each other apart!

Katrina walked by them. She sat lonely in a cracking white bench.

Maralyn felt that she didn't know what Katrina wanted, or what exactly she should say to her.

"Mindfuck" by Da$h featuring J.I.D. played from the other girl's earphones now. It was turned up loud enough for the original pair to be able to discern its outline.

Then, she walked around seemingly very bored–but with something inside keeping her excited. And that maybe inner fire glided her around the dirt. Or maybe it was water. She just didn't trot; she rarely did.

Reaching Maralyn, away from the boy's line of hearing, she inquired about if they had been gossiping about her.

"No," Maralyn replied. "But he seemed very mad about you,"

She furrowed her brows, saying, "What do you mean? Trevor always does this. He talks about me but then falls for me when I see him the next day,"

"What do you mean?" Maralyn asked her.

"I don't know. Like. I remember one time he called me his wind-up dancer, or some shit–like–his tiny dancer,"

Maralyn clenched her lips into a small circle and rose her eyebrows, amused.

Eyes were on Katrina. Her shoulders were like gentle mountains supporting her lowly and strong neck–and every movement, everywhere, she looked, was graceful. Baby pink Vans shoes accentuated her dark under-eyes. An altar boy on the porch took a sip of coffee, watching her from above his cup. Some kids kicked a kickball ball around in the courtyard, just waiting to get yelled at.

The girl had no idea, she didn't realize, how magical and important she seemed. To Maralyn, to Trevor, to many.

To her, beauty was never about ego; deep down, love was not about power. Regardless of society and its norms–now or former. Having smoked wax last night, in a realer world, she leaned back and fluttered her eyes out at space.

Chapter 21

Katrina glares upward into the big screen. She feels as if the boy is looking back at her. She doesn't know where he is, she doesn't know if he is really doing it.

I know you well. she thinks–towards him.

Does she?

Does she? How fucking boring are you, the screen boy thinks back, millions, thousands of miles away. From foreign places up, down, left, right–diagonally, oscillating, crossing in fragmented lines and spheres, layers overlapping.

Wow! I'm so fucking cool! This is everything I've ever wanted… I'm so smart, I should get a scholarship, right now.

Katrina gets fed up, grabbing an old remote the size of her forearm and squashing the power button, essentially breaking it.

After this, she strolls for a little in the black-and-white space.

It is grey, a greyish blue or greyish green space; she walks until she hits a wall with her head. Katrina then reaches her home, peaceful point. It was like another wall, except that she is contentedly staring at it.

"If I'm God, are you Satan?" she says out loud. Directed towards a figurative, fluorescent Maralyn.

Suddenly, Josiah comes into mind. Her body momentarily pauses on his glittering qualities of talent and innocence. His piano skills, things which his best friend ignored, his family situation.

I mean, I say that because I decided that you are no longer the counterpart to my Angel. You are not my Demon, my omen, she thinks.

Her eyes close. They develop into black, dark ovals against the oiliness of her face. She had been neglecting her nightly face wash.

"And her soul died in her for fear: she knew she had never seen him, he had never seen her, they had met in the dark and had fought in the dark, not knowing whom they met nor whom they fought."
–D.H. Lawrence - "The Odour of Chrysanthemums"

Misery

°Curse of the girls° Rosie Tweeted.

It was random, but Maralyn felt like it probably precipitated from some drama in her social life. That was the kind of person she was.

It was 7:42pm on an exhausted Tuesday.

4 people from the group had gathered to smoke weed a few hours before. Maralyn and Katrina joined later, riding in the back with Brett and Jesse now to Dakota's house.

Streaked across the sky, on an intense, bright billboard, was the sentence:

Don't confuse the screen lights with the holy light.

Katrina's head bobbed forward as she registered the words.

She felt as if it was something important, almost mystical. The scent of gas was pungent with each turn as the west wind dragged it into the car.

Maralyn silently agreed, taking in the stimuli and accepting the harrowing rush of their lives.

It's all nonsensical, she thought.

Like an autotuned ghost, words entered both of the girls' minds: "The wise and elderly man with the long, mountainous beard."

"Fear is a voice in your head. There will be no voices in your head." The last words he speaks are "Are you scared?"

Chapter 22

The other side, the other face, is to the "big screen" looking at us through the camera.

We think.

A lot of what we show is inspired by wanting to please the base reactions of people like the little boy. He represents all that we can remember of who has truly judged us, scared us.

Thrilled us, loved us.

The log said Josiah had entered a day and a half ago.

°you think youre just immune to it all?° Katrina sent to Maralyn, seeing that she was online.

°But like, what have I done wrong°

Sent as she was typing the "done," the girl replied, °im just trying to help you°

Maralyn took in a deep sigh.

She then decided that she would take a break from the argument. There were Scooby Doo fruit snacks in the pantry and she simply had to go grab some. Hunkered down on her phone, she saw that Jesse Tweeted eight minutes ago:

°middleton kids tho°

Even bigger sigh. A long thought process ensued.

She felt guilty in light of her spoiledness, a facet that was probably an eternal truth, but still angry at what that message could mean in her friendships. Heated conversations which were really fights–inflamed struggles of the subliminal.

What did you do to have an ego like that? she thought. Twitter word is not bond.

Maralyn didn't want these telepathic stabs at the heart in her life any longer, especially when they posed as helpful gestures. But as much as she hated them, she would do her best to be more considerate. Of the less privileged.

"I'm just trying to help you,"

The program was glitchingly upside-down now, yet the messages still maintained the correct orientation.

It was when the rest of the structure was revealed, a literal fog being lifted from its edges and poles, that one could tell that it was a school Smartboard. Like the ones in most Sigma classrooms.

"I'm really starting to hate you all," the boy spoke. "I really am,"

And there was no joke, no music, no art piece to provide relief for his condition.

yuh…yah

On a bench on the A level, near Sigma.

Oh, oh, she thought. They're watching me.

She put on her bulky knit has so as to hide some of her face, and develop a feeling of protection around her head.

Surely they're watching me… It's hot in here. I wish I had a friend,

To her it was like… they were watching her. Like she or Katrina or Josiah might do behind one of the Screens, glaring up and ruining their eyes and brains. She calmly, or that was the attempt, sank lower into the chair and gulped. She was about to take out her phone to go on vsco, but she felt that the crowd would nonverbally judge her usage of it. The way she turned her thumbs, minorly moved her eye movements, reddened in the face. Even though they could barely see the details of her body. The edges of the chair towered over her at this point, and most people were hunched over their activities.

Okay, it's going got be okay, she reassured herself, once again merely trying, then her world reached a chaotic stasis.

An hour, of ruminating and sweating, and went by and Maralyn exited the area. She vaguely saw the shadow of a yellow light spinning in front of her. When she reached the destination, unknowingly following it, she sat on the ground. In the middle.

"Hey there," the voice spoke.

Her body shook up: a chill slowly yet urgently raining down her ribs.

"What's up?" Then, in a tone more calm, "How are you?"

His inflection dripped from the walls, the words tumbling over one another like in a drunken fight or loud stadium. But his gentleness sounded oddly heroic.

"What?" she responded.

"Take out those headphones first, will you,"

"Oh," she replied blankly, still in shock. "Well I'm doing good. And yourself?"

How the fuck did I get here, she thought.

"You're just going to have to sit down and…uh, bear with me. If you'd like to."

Jesus christ, she thought. "Okay, sure,"

"I was called here. Don't ask me by who, and especially not what. Not those questions, don't do it please. Anyways, I was just sent over here to talk with you for a little. Maralyn. Have a nice little chat about love and priorities, or whatever you need, and whatever. So just open up to me for a little before you go to Heather's house, and I promise I can help you out. But I'm gonna need you to calm down first, breathe, sit in this chair."

A chair magically appeared in the white room.

"And just for your information, I'm also dead, but don't worry about it. I'm not going to hurt you, I don't wanna. The opposite actually, but anyways, let's talk,"

"Dude what even is your name? Your voice sounds so familiar, like it's my dad's or something…but first of all my dad's not fucking dead, and he has an accent, and that would just be disturbing to say the least. Or my uncle? Shit. This is weird, and I really was not nice to him… Fuck–"

"Buddy, calm down,"

And at once she was calm.

"What's been bothering you?"

"Oh, okay," she responded. "Well since you're my therapist,"

The figure rolled his imaginary eyes, extra-puffing on a cigarette.

"So here this is," Maralyn began. She kept zoning in and out during the near monologue, but retained focus during the important moments. The voice listened to every word.

"There's this person in my life. A friend, a sort of ex-loved one slash romantic interest, ex? I don't know. We dated for a little a while back; it ended weirdly. It's a girl, and her and I don't talk personally a lot, but I feel like when we do it's usually me initiating conversation. Anyways, fast forward, and I think I'm still…in love with her. Or in infatuation. But it's the same feeling as when we met, and it was all innocent then, and not obsessive or too sexual. I don't know,

"But I find myself doing strange things, not acting like myself, to get her attention or approval. It sucks, this whole feeling in me feels like a trap. Something is wrong and maybe somebody out there can help me get rid of it. Honestly, I've been observing her from afar and admiring it all, and just been stuck in 'she loves me, she loves me not.' I think, I tried to let go. I was moving on. But she always comes back, this lover of mine, dressing up all nicely and having fun with Josiah and stuff. Also getting to know people who I don't really like anymore. Always coming around. And there's her flirtatious vibes, which isn't too frequent I'm not gonna lie, but she'll just touch my hand or something in a hallway or a dark place, and I never really remember it afterwards. It's almost like ghost moments. But the feeling is there…the same feeling from when we were together. Same with her social media presence, it's like all shadows and echoes of that time. She hasn't seemed the exact same since.

"I don't even care about any of this really, I just want to know what happened; and how she feels. Or felt. And how I feel. Like, what can I do with myself? I'm scared, and maybe you were sent here for me, because every time I do try to talk meaningfully with her or her close friends, it's like they shut me off or hide or something. It's weird, it leads me to this sad or depressing vibe. Does any of that make sense? I just want two people to embrace their feelings."

"It makes total sense," he responded. "Thank you for sharing it,"

Maralyn replied: "Of course, I should be thanking you. I already feel kind of better…and more clear about it, almost,"

She continued, "But anyhow. She means a lot to me. I think I will try to articulate these feelings and thoughts better to her soon. Before it's "too late" I guess, and before senior year starts and everyone gets older or graduates.

"Love is one of my priorities, so is truth. One time I wrote in my journal, a few weeks ago, "the truth is in battle with love." Is that so? But can they live together as one? Is peace possible? What is true peace? It matters, right? This world is so lost and confused. But I'm hoping with the help of friends like you, I can make it better before I leave it. We can, together."

He said, "There's something I kind of identify with, and I'd like to share it with you."

The essence took a drag from his cigarette. "Beneath lovers, there is always friendship. That comes with "true love." The friendship can be there in really strange, weird, distant ways, right? But it's still love. Especially if you know it is."

"I think I'm understanding," she replied.

"Friends come and go. What I want to say is, trust your intuition. What's inside of you and what's not. Let that love and light guide you; you can and will walk along the path that leads you to love and truth. Because those are the treasures of your heart, and life, man! And the gold is in the flooring, the proof is in the air, in all the waves you speak of and dream of.

"Well," Maralyn responded / in awe.

"Goddamn, you're making me miss that crazy, confusing shit a little! It's hard to attach to another in heaven. The souls are separated. But we're still in paradise. At least for me, buddy. Anyways, you can think about that when you're ready, I'm sorry… You guys are young and full of vitality."

He went on.

"We're becoming one now, do you see it? Just like the dead and living unite at the end of slow, lazy Sunday nights. Love and truth will find their place, peacefully fitting next to each other. In body and mind. I'm not scared anymore. Just keep enjoying what music you do now, there are better songs when you arrive here. Don't be excited for death, but there are so many beautiful sonic rivers that run through these terrifying pockets of darkness here."

"Okay," Maralyn responded firmly.

"Las thing I'll tell you is… Love that girl. Push away your fear. Look at it, and then ignore it. Recognize the things that terrify you and remember to look away to the light. Be loving, be you. Be free. Well, anyways, my name is Kurt Cobain." he said with an all-knowing smile and chuckle. "And you just got punk'd! No, no. No,"

"Dude!" the girl freaked out. "That's insane. I'm honored,"

"Yup, that would be me. Uh, I mean, it's me. That's me. Man, whatever lol,"

"Wha– H–how…did you just say 'lol' out loud?"

"Well, what do you mean?"

"Like, how did you just say the acronym out loud? We all read it in our heads, but like differently. How did it just come into my brain like that? As if it was texted to me," she continued. "I'm so confused, my guy…"

"Maralyn, it isn't fucking important," he said.

"Oh yeah!" she exclaimed, chuckling nervously. "True. But wait, holy shit, how are you doing this? Do you talk to Jim Morrison? Does that mean I get to talk to him? And how are you, by the way? I really liked Bleach and In Utero, and Incesticide. This is all really crazy, man! All I was doing was talking to you about Katrina,"

"Thank you, for everything," he simply replied, in his gravelly, grumbly tone.

"Of course! Thank you for talking to me, I think it's really made a change. I think I will go somewhere with this, after this,"

"You're all good. That's why I was sent here, for you and kids like you. Just focus on yourself, yeah? And the ones that you love?"

"Yeah, sure thing; I think I know what you mean."

The subsequent silence was serene and loving. But, she instinctively knew that he was to go soon.

"Until next time,"

"Of course."

"Bye, you,"

"And by the way, I'm still dead,"

"Shit."

A long, but warm, silence ensued.

"Okay well, sounds good," she added. "I will go now. Bye now. Bye for now, friend,"

It hurt her to pick up her backpack and remember the space turning off. How it was necessary, how it needed to. How their was a life to live beyond it, to truly jump inside, populate, habituate. But she'd have to do it, and she would. People would take the place of her ghost friends, hopefully. With a snug fit, maybe even honoring their memory too. Their dead memory.

"And, by the way again, Maralyn… Don't smoke too much weed. And keep on running. Run. Run forever."

Dwing! It turned off. The girl was off to her friend's house, scheduled to hop inside Jesse's car in 5 minutes.

Form is the End

So this was it, huh.

"Special" and embeaned with qualities fit for a renaissance painter's master, not the painter, besides the glow of a family fire. According to the family. The friends. She Snapchatted, and she emailed, and she recorded, and where did her art classes lead her but to a short form, paradoxical, grammatically errored existence? Josiah, her supposed best friend Jay, was almost gone now, and so was smoothies at the mall and Thursday studying and Starbucks. Left her, oh right, that's what it was, left you; and even though her family was present, she was gone, too.

Red-orange flower petals cradled in bright green stems to contrast with the hunter of the trees. Or was it just their leaves, and really they were black inside? Several little brown. The sun–"I am the trees." Because he peeked in. Oh, because they all peeked in. And she didn't. And she peeked in first. And she didn't! Because, even though she was there, she didn't. It was all just mirrors and particles and forms of light rays and wavelengths and projections and echoes, but it was not actually real. There were realizations that have been guiding her life, no matter since how young (*so* young), and it was her taking them and making conclusions. This happens to everyone supposedly, but not her.

Sociology. The years in which she spent in high school, in your country, in your region. Sociology; anthropology. Theories of sociology she read summarized through a blogger's worldview: she read and scanned when nobody was looking and she told the stories to herself.

She hung with them before she could figure it out.

Maybe, maybe oh evolving civilization, beloved of millions, she decided on something after seeing that since there were so many answers, there were actually none. Free will–a social construct like all the rest of the terms–was fabricated, a creation by a (somehow long-dead, almost never-existed) God who had human interests nowhere in mind, when they created it, a concept to trip over everybody interested. Somebody working behind a video game. People interested in modern sociology and accessibly written online psychology articles. And her, and her friends, were resolved as a part of destiny. Some goddamn destiny: a continually unstable, crumbling idea of energy. And it absolutely had nothing to do with her at all. And her friends.

Maralyn sat and thought now. The night was hers, every night was hers. And she only did so about Katrina. Her favorite girl–she saw her golden, tan skin now and imagined her light eyes cushioned in it. Here were her ideas…:

You don't deserve to be bombarded by information. Emails, texts, calls, status updates–even though you're so good at making your family like you–it's all the same! Repeat and repeat. Rinse, wish, do it all again, please the same people. But once again, you are good at doing it, because you are a good person. I wonder how many people have told you that you're just a good, kind person, worthy of love and care… Maybe I'm just projecting, though, Lord knows I need that message.

Maralyn's thoughts went on while the shower ran.

I will be the person to be there like that, as needed like they say in medicine (Maralyn recalled her mother's nursing job), and without want for reciprocating or more of you. More more more, everything is so delicious and yummy! Like the lovers always do but their desires are endless. And gross.

Katrina. You taught me to stand still and be calm. Somehow, I don't even know if I can live up to these promises…but when I look at you, look back at you and forwards, I see an angel placed on the wrong planet or society, because somehow I know that you have been my own reminder for good all this time. I didn't even know it, no one did or does.

The noises downstairs in her house grew louder, as if synced to Maralyn's thoughts. Perhaps they were actively transmitting, like she was impulsively texting or Tweeting them all out, allowing anybody on Earth to tap in.

You were there, even when I didn't know I needed it. You were something sable, a real hand to hold onto. And what I did, Katrina–

She walked to her mirror.

I turned you into one of my virtual, dream fantasies. I made you into my own sort of hologram, and I just wanted to be next to you the entire time. Because I thought that it would be my medicine, my remedy. For the psychopath shit that I've been through, that's engrained in my past and reality. Well, let's just call it insane.

The thoughts began to experience like shadows, some genre of echoes.

No, back when we were dating, it was you who guided me into my truth, the truth that I am not crazy, I am just human. And two people have equal parts in making something better and having each others' backs. You taught me that from you character and demeanor. Katrina… If you could hear all this right now, I would say that…

Maralyn, in her bathroom, shifted around.

I should've done my part more, and thank God it's not too late to make up for lost joyfulness, humanity, and lost hope, too. Because my only wish is that you see me for who I am again, not even remembering anything or glorifying, and trust that I will be a better soulmate to you. I'm going to fuck up, I'm going to make mistakes, I know I am–but will you forgive me? Will you see me for me?

I wish I knew you better, I do, the girl thought as she stared down her moist red palms–but for now I have to trust you and succeed with my plans in life. Whatever these are…no matter how the Projects turn out.

The slow-moving girl turned out the light as if it were a disease, then headed back to her bedroom.

But she realized one more thing before retreating to bed. And, she'd actually most likely fall asleep well tonight–because of safety, understanding, and a sensation of all-enveloping love. Don't stop now, a voice in her mind told her.

You were just human.

Jokes on me, she quietly thought. Just like me.

This entire time.

The girl shuffled Kid Cudi's "Man On The Moon: The End Of Day" on low volume for the soothing instrumentals and then fell asleep. She had whispered "I don't feel dirty anymore" to the Universe as it played.

Chapter 23

But then; impulsively. Obsessively. A kickflip. An extraordinary demonstration, betrayal of faith.

There could be seen, from even the far side, a titanic pool of fury in Josiah's eyes. It was a magnetic fire, just like the one that bound Maralyn's knee into Trevor's gut–sparking him to scurry away. Katrina had cried then.

Josiah landed a hotfisted jab to Maralyn's face, who insisted on moving forward then, causing it to crash into her left eye.

A floor of lava. Reminders of idle time, hallway games. Warm plates. Foreign pathways and bridges–meant for therapy and somewhat spiritualistic ritual of the body.

Maralyn. Calmly closed her eyes. They felt warm. The fight, the day, were meant for more. The fight of the day did not offer more. Calmly closed her eyes, kept them. It was relaxing, sort of…

Jay's mouth was agape, and he began to stare at Maralyn; and then Katrina.

He patiently, with his eternally collected mind, reflected on the two. Turned around. Began pacing the circular spot. Turned his back on them. The wall was cold.

"This is everything that happens, that is happening, between us," Maralyn remembered hearing herself say in a dream last night.

"I finally," she muttered, quizzically, now. "I finally made a move,"

Things. "I don't know." Real. Anxiety.

Faint music played from a surround sound system, which they began to hear now.

Blood dripping from Maralyn's nose and jaw. There was nausea. In everybody.

The ultimate feeling, or something, really, began to peak for Maralyn.

She slowly pointed her head down–her shiny forehead accentuated. With all of the knowledge and wit inside her ego, Maralyn picked up the gun behind her backpack.

It had landed there, she noticed that, about twenty minutes ago, or twenty centuries ago. It was soft and beautiful, in a monstrous way, with the handle clenched in her right fist.

"There is no heat," Katrina said. "Or coldness,"

The teardrops forming beneath Katrina's squinting eyes could have threatened her strong, superior, dominant, alpha position. So she quickly shook her head to rid them.

Josiah's enemy, Maralyn, checked on her face before doing anything about the gun. He scanned for: insecurity, weakness, loopholes. The boy with the long hair. The power powder, the weapon, the destruction.

He pouted.

Maralyn's shoulders were up straight, and her back fierce against whatever draft threatened to shift her movement.

Josiah looked at all in disgust.

Katrina was pouting now, too. Her eyes were shiny, like a clean and clear mirror reflecting an insecure person, but also pure. The purity, almost a naivety, an innocent code of morals.

But not ethics. Jack White would have been screaming.

Katrina didn't nod or say yes, but her aura seemed to speak for her: "You know what do do."

After a bizarrely patient pause from Katrina (Maralyn would judge it later), Maralyn said, "Only you,"

Okay then, Maralyn thought, looking at Josiah and Maralyn confidently.

Her arm rose, pointing at her best friend, and her index finger closed into her.

It was completed.

°The good memories were so short. Compared to everything else, at least.° Sage Tweeted, and then locked his phone screen.

His room smelled like the Adidas shop he visited last weekend in Brooklyn due to all of the open shoe boxes. He was pleased with his purchases, sleeping well at night knowing how cool he'd look to girls and ex-friends in these coming weeks.

He had remained a simple boy, having tightly grasped his self, and couldn't have been more proud of his accomplishments. He scored an A on his community service Project, and finished his video in time to just perform shenanigans for a little while. So him and his friend since childhood Kensington (Kenny) drove to New York.

°But everything makes sense now, oddly enough° he added to the website.

Blindly Watching

Bubbles on the ground.

Bubbles to the ground. Bubbles in the green; iridescent purple and light pink and baby blue forms, together on the pavement and beyond. Their eyes created it wherever; their serenity and mistakes ensured that it worked. Their points, whether shallow and rattling or as high as Everest, made it all work.

Henry's voice. To Rosie… Rosie. Henry's gentle, yet jesting, voice of cranberry chocolate; maybe he was depressed inside and maybe he wasn't. He was a great boy, to her and Dakota and Jesse, either way.

He, or somebody, seemed to have said something indistinct or unclear. To Katrina, it seemed.

Insecurities

The boy calmly stares at the window, his eyes pacing the road with no cars right to left and left to right. He sat in his uncomfortable wooden desk chair. Dad finally left, but Mom was yelling at something or someone.

Everything is going to be okay, he thought.

The girls reflected on the pink sky up ahead. Its clouds could be equated with cotton candy fluffs, or simply bunches of sweet nothing.

Katrina sat on her porch, her chair silver yet seemingly rusting for until the end of time. Circled by the stripe cushion coated chairs, their glass table seemed antiquated, but familiar. She loved her house because it was everything that her mother wanted and liked. Angular, simply sweet, warm. After her restless father came into their life again, in middle age, they added the last touches.

He just doesn't give a shit, she thought once the man came to mind. My brownass dad,

Or so it seemed to her.

A development in life experience might have proved her just wrong and confused. Something could allow a shift in that familial perspective, a type of event rooted in that journey people talk of when they say the word “miracle.”

To be cut off.

I wonder the ways in which I'd turn out to be like him, if I become a parent.

She wanted to always use "when" instead of "if," but thinking about her high school love life often sent her down a long, spiraling road. Of imagining that she would be a horrible wife and mother. And she did not want to commence on that tonight.

Next.

Maralyn lied flat on the grass. Her brother, massaging their cousin’s new puppy, sat to her right. The dog ran off, back and forth along the path of Clara’s wet tennis ball. Elias had laid out a beach towel for them to cover the soggy ground, but their butts still received brown water prints.

The evening's soft stratus allowed the separate girls to be enveloped in dreams of their own. This was all mutual in the best of all possible worlds. Everybody was gay with a certain type of happiness. History would read a party if everybody just got their right portion of juice, beyond one night.

Suddenly Maralyn remembered the words Katrina had spoke at the end of her dream about killing Josiah:

"I never wanted you to do that. Hurting other people hurts me,"

Now I'm sad, Maralyn thought. But shit is fucked,

Life is fucked. This is just how things are; I guess how they'll be everywhere and forever.

Telling me, telling me, Josiah ruminated at least three thousand times in that one sitting.

The same things over and over,

Informing me. Feeding me.

My parents, friends, the schools, careers, the future, the past, the great and eternal present. There is no parents, fuck parents. Because everything is infinity, everything happens so nothing happens.

After every pause, he labeled these ideas as angsty, and so cringy, but the cold of his depression kept him moving forward. And besides (although he didn't realize it now), there was no time for people's judgments–if there ever was. He heard yells between his parents from downstairs. Josiah felt cynically empathetic towards those kids evacuated from a sense of safe reality due to their parents' marginal, petty arguments. Or maybe he would understand them when he got older, but he wished that he wouldn't.

He was not chanting anthems, he was finally communicating with himself; no reflection around and no soul to relay the damages to. Or to be present for intervention, essentially a challenge from them at this point. After today, no matter what went down, the external world would not matter anymore. He had found his true self, held the ego, and tossed all good or bad emotions down a dirty drain. Although his face was stone, his blood was still fluid.

And the cheeks switched from red to blue as he set up the rope. He had tested the bar by gathering large rocks from the pond near Opifer and then hanging a filled, sturdy backpack from it.

Some of his last words were, recited out loud,

"I had to eat you all before you eat me."

Chapter 24

Katrina didn't write much, but she calmly recorded poetry tonight in an old math notebook.

She daydreamt about a singer like Jesse's blue vocals (recalling that one song that Trevor and Maralyn made together) and some simple drums. These stanzas were interspersed over three pages and sandwiched with scribbles. Her room smelled like trees and rose oil, which she really enjoyed that night.

"Very changing
Time is slowing down as it runs out
They have my ear at every word
And I told you,
I was hungry
Now

I fall, she comes, I sleep
And awake, now
We can come back to all this later
to all this later, girls and boys
You can escape me, that's easy,
but you can't ever escape you
You will never leave the whirlpool of repetition
until it drowns you.

What's growing on you?
I'd tell a foreigner
out of all the things here, you will only get used to the temperature.
Forever oblivious through oblivion"

Now I need a good cry. Now it's kind of hitting…like a high, she thought.

And randomly: There comes a point during becoming close with someone that their facial features sort of disappear. You suddenly only see their eyes and not the very position in which their eyes are placed. And you find yourself having forgotten about all the acne on their skin. Or their clothing choices.

I hope everything will be okay.

It will. I know it will.

Trigger warning

"We currently have breaking news that, once again, there *is* an active shooter at Monico High School near Dayton, Ohio. Our sources say that the rampage began around 12:13, while half the students were at lunch, and the east wing is the one affected. As you can see from the helicopter view, the town is sending in as much personnel as it can get and SWAT teams are rushing in. Students from the main wing are *evacuating* and just being told to run, run away as fast as they can at this time; and as you can see, distraught parents are crying with their loved ones and reuniting on a field nearby. It is a chaotic situation, and questions are already trending on social media about gun control and our government system, as you can see shared on our Facebook and Twitter right now."

°what the fuck is going on omfg. this country is crazy.° Rosie Tweeted.

°so fucked up

i fucking hate america. this only happens here° °all my regards and prayers to the students and people affected in dayton°

°This is surreal° Trevor contributed.

"Hahaha," the boy voiced. "That's what your ass gets."

The comfort of his navy blue cotton jacket helped him ignore the cacophony of deafening screams in the hallway.

"Take that," And his body turned right with his left arm flexing a bit more. The gun fired two times, right in the face of a girl and in the abdomen of a girl running.

They all meet in the middle, through me. he thought while moving around. Not God or Satan, but a pure, neutral harbringer of necessary destruction…nature, at its finest, the protector of death. We all meet in my world on this great day. My little world which is not simple or naïve; it is a tornado sent from my own inner soul. I can show these all every single possibility, in their opportunistic, puny lives.

And hahahaha, he laughed, they all knew that we were going to haunt each other.

He unintentionally began to speak out loud, almost shouting. His pupils were tiny, and surrounded by black and grey clouds ruining his blue irises. The teenager's, looking like an adult now, body appeared stiff and ugly. It was indeed strained, this was unnatural for his age and time. Plus, he'd end up in prison afterwards if he didn't shoot himself, too.

"It is my time, it has come. I will spare the strong, smart, great, beautiful, naturally separating themselves from the rest of the vermin… God bless America. Here in this school, I was guarantee and guard Amendment number 1, we will let the people speak and continue to do so. No corrupt insect will stifle these deep, core birthrights. Haha, I should have been a teacher,

Those who have ignored my style and intellectual cadence must and shall feel and learn, as children do, be shown, their wrongs. To never make the same mistakes again. I will reign! Hahaha! I. Will. Reign!"

Students there would later comment that the previous monologue sounded extremely indecipherable and mumbled at the time. But the sick shooter seemed very passionate about it. And those who knew him would admit that they had no idea the mental struggles he must have been going through before the event.

Take *that*, you little bitch, he said–back in his mind again. Go fuck yourself! he thought towards a freshman boy making a shell over a petite blonde girl, the one underneath staring him directly in the face.

"What?" he ironically asked them. He flipped his gun on the pair.

Both of their bodies shuddered, the boy's fragmented whimpers audible now. But before hitting the trigger, he realized that he wanted to shoot elsewhere.

I don't know, his thoughts went. That is what you get, bitch. And now you all look at me! Why is that? Is that crazy?

"What the fuck do you want from me?" he shouted towards every person in view. "Stop yelling at me,"

Human nature is so fucking weird. he thought as he turned a corner,

The teenager stared down, as if into a numbing, joy-filled oasis.

A fleeting, but very clear, image of his freshman year biology classroom passed through his mind. First he hated it and wanted it to disappear (he shot another one, it was loud and surprising which was great), next he stammered the thought away by a wild flame of the eyes. He acted on the feeling of power and fear enacted by his demeanor by firing the gun four more times. The third was interspersed from the second, when he nearly tripped on a girl's body while reaiming at a door's rectangle window. He ended the spree, cascade, crusade by cleanly firing into a crowd.

The smell of sour bodily fluids atop notes of gunpowder and smoking wood permeated the hallway on nearly every floor. It was incredibly pungent and disturbing. The screams grew louder by the second, even though the episode was over.

I hope you know we're terrified, Macy, a chunky Latina girl of fifteen, thought as she shakily looked for his face. And you know what, we're gonna be traumatized forever, if this is what you wanted,

She simply hoped in this moment that she would make it out alive; she texted her mother I love yous for the family, just in case.

He noticed her searching and wanted to spit or stomp on her. But his target began to involve. The girl and her family's prayers were answered, either darkly or happily; the target morphed into people who looked like him.

The poor kids, he thought. All of these. No protection, nobody to shield them.

He still wanted war, complete and total war; he went in expecting that feeling. At the end, he realized that this was all available inside of him. As he walked past his victims, he realized it would be a miracle if he had just set the precedent for a centuries-long exchange of revenge and human power. Battles and wars. Multiple sides crashing against one another like hurricane winds, the final destination would be natural annihilation, the end of the earth, hell, the angels and black.

But the hope and doom definitively clashed inside of him–making even certain that the end result would not be good.

The assailant paced up the stairs, then looked around at the hallway landing. He saw a seemingly safe spot next to the windows and took it. He rested the handgun at his belt to above his right ear.

Right before pulling the trigger, he thought: I am so lucky.

°Jesus christ, this country is ridiculous. Our politicians only cater to companies that lobby for them and persuade them. And that's why no change gets done every time something like this happens° Henry Tweeted, immediately receiving 6 Retweets and 14 Likes.

°remember, that it could have been us°

"Monico is supposedly one of most renown public high schools in the state. The graduation rate is 95% and the racial make-up 71% white, 25% black, and the rest other. But we have just received news that a suspect has been identified; it is a 16 year old Caucasian male who was homeschooled but involved in clubs and sports in the area.

A few students at the school said that they played video games *with* him, communicating online through 4chan and other forums…noting that his username was "th3_bigboy2590" as you can see from the screenshots behind me. The suspect has been described as highly reclusive and *sheltered*. It is currently unknown if he is in custody or still in the area where the massacre occurred. Online records suggest that the…boy had been seeing a therapist for schizophrenia and bipolar related problems, about 5 months before his rampage. But he stopped once he was placed on medication by his doctors, and was on, uh, a plethora of medications." A moment went by. "Uh, we will, uh, be providing updates as the situation develops, while parents still find their children and police forces protect the campus from any secondary attacks."

Chapter 25

"*I Bathe In Hate*"

Bright green lights. Stage. A base of neutral green with a riffing cascade of neon. Punk energy integrated by steady, calculating fingers into an adolescent genre's history.

Baggy jeans; beige cap with a semi-flattened bill, an indecipherable logo; yellow t-shirt; worn-out grey Adidas. The models with millions of followers on social media–posed next to skinny figures who had been posing with guns the year before.

But still, the power of the youth. That night. An abundance of hyper, quiet teenagers–girls and boys–roamed around a restaurant booth. It was by the border of a wet parking lot, and containing a figure in this outfit. The shadow emitted by the very booth he sat in was darker than his hooded brows, his black skin. His fingers typed out another exclamatory call for union into his device, through subspaces, ready for anybody with an Internet connection.

When a girl in a pink sweatshirt and ripped jeans approached him, like a shy cat, to show him something on her phone or at least take a photo–he merely put his head down, playing with his shoelaces and chuckling.

"*Please Be Real.*"

Katrina had sunk into the pillow chair inside her bedroom. She had been scrolling social media for hours, looking for updates in the situation, keeping up with those affected, and distracting herself when things got overwhelming.

Often finding solace in fashion and music accounts, she delved into Ian Connor's Twitter for an hour, at one point. She had overheard from Trevor and Rosie a few weeks before that he had allegations of rape released against him. She was unsure of their current status or the court case (if any), but took everything with a grain of salt. She had to, as a girl, a young woman. And as a person of color, which she had learned in a YouTube educational series, were more at risk of sexual assault than white folks. Katrina had friends with lives forever changed by the mindless actions of abusers.

Still, the man's personal life, especially intimate, was of neither her interest or business. She stalked his profiles because they seemed like art galleries, made up of cultural combinations in words, outfits, and photography. "Separate art from the artist" was a futile phrase, another little mantra, because the definition of viewer posited that the person view the art. Regardless of the artist's own life. Most art did not require, and even discouraged, knowing the artist on a personal level in order to enjoy it. These were simply her beliefs; she knew that they would incite rage by many if she vocalized them.

Plus, she did not know enough about the girl or girls affected by Ian's actions. She had also seen that the boy himself had denied the allegations, also seeing claims that they were fabricated by a twisted enemy. There were too many details. Mainly, she did not personally know enough of the people involved. Realizing that she knew none of them, she settled with enjoying everybody's art. This was comfortable for her, as it conformed to the very idea of art and its audience. And why else was she still alive besides art?

Katrina could give and take, she could stand up for herself. She was smart and strong enough for compromise. Consideration. Balance. Understanding. Mainly, she did not need Twitter and Tumblr hives to voice and defend her ethics for her.

She hated war.

A good distraction, a positive distraction, work like Ian's art pages were during world events such as these.

Horrific, monstrous acts, en masse. It was all horrible. She set her heart on that day forward to art.

Before She Heard the News

9pm. Maralyn sat at home, scribbling throughout her journals, having left school early because it was the end of the year anyways and she decided to give up on the final exams. Her and Josiah's Project song had been completed, with Trevor's help, two weeks ago. So she decided to write a letter to a friend.

"I'm so sorry, for the hurt and confusion and fear I've caused you in life. I had a crazy dream recently and realized I had to reconnect with you. I don't ever want to lose you as a friend, mainly. Katrina. I took you for granted the moment I met you, I couldn't look up and see you in the eyes. There is a cord, some kind of indestructible wire or rope, made out of light and stardust and God's own original ingredients (or something) and the entire Universe, which keeps me bound to you. I am so thankful that the first thing I felt when I saw your body was fear, because it's taught and reminded me that this is all real. You are not a planet, you are just my soul's planet. I think that cord from before is called eternity, or forever."

When writing, Maralyn had to swallow the discomfort she experienced upon writing out her name and then giving it back to her. It still felt cathartic, like a release.

"Furthermore, the thing is… you appeared to me before I knew your name or shape. It was like I manifested you, or I received a vision of you. All I knew was, at age 14 then (gross): "I need someone, I need a boy or girl here" not necessarily to save me from myself or my demons or something crazy - but just to hold next to me and be held by. I reached out, felt you, I saw the outline of your breathing. And you gave me hope in my depression even then.

I don't know why this all is. Any of this, including this letter and our ups and downs and vices and moments of joy. Remembering your presence in this Universe and world saves me while on the brink of existence, every time, it seems. I can never get enough of you either, even though lust is pretty much futile, and I can never get over you. Whenever you make me sad or anxious, and such."

Maralyn noticed that the communication was getting long, but it felt right. She did not want to force anything.

"I hope too much of this didn't sound really illusory or dreamy or exaggerated. You matched the healing energy that was needed for my unfair youthful depression. And you distracted me and saved me, preventing my body from deteriorating and my soul from disappearing forever. You became that forever…no, you just solved it. And more things. And I'm forever indebted to you. Now that I've met MY own god, I finally understand that it's okay to feel what I feel, and express my true self. (I hope I am not my own god, or that I assume so). So there is my truth, and my "love," completely layed out for you here. It's just something.

Now I know that part of the hope you've given me maybe had to do with the idea of being with you. Like being with you hypothetically, and being genuinely dating or getting know each other compared to what we slightly experienced. I feel like I never really go to know you, and have just been addicted this whole time without any genuine pure experience, or personal closure/knowledge."

That was it. For now. She sealed it up and placed it into an old greeting card envelope, a pastel green one. She was excited to give it to her, finally content with words to the girl.

Chapter 26

The kids felt destabilized, almost paralyzed, while heading into school today. Most of them decided to go through the main entrance, sharing warm moments, distracting themselves. There was a general incontinence in the air, which contrasted with the uppity auras that the lobby usually welcomed. Maralyn walked with a heaviness. A certain phrase was engrained in her mind, then. "This is fucked up; so fucked up." And she was scared. Josiah was too. They all were. But students could still be seen walking around, shouting and giving high-fives.

A bake sale to raise funds for a summer program was even being run. Dakota and Jesse stopped by to purchase brownies and other classics. Josiah never made an appearance that day. Katrina arrived 10 minutes late, a confused Opifer populace still roaming around, listening to the band Daughter. Nobody wanted to go to class, nobody wanted to manage class.

But towards the end of the school day, Maralyn caught up to Katrina to gently give her the letter. She knew where her long-time crush would be, her mind sadly followed these directions whenever it was time to part ways. She knew that one day this would have to stop, and she *would* make it so, but she always felt a meaning behind it. She didn't know what it was, but the intuition was there. Today, that aspect of the obsession made sense. She knew that after their 4th period together, Katrina would head off to geography class alongside Christina. And so she handed her it then. The hallway was loud, jumbled, chaotic, despite the morning's hush–but everything came to a standstill again because they were sharing an important moment. Together; finally.

Katrina accepted the package with a friendly smile, but was moderately confused. When Maralyn walked away she wondered, why would she give it to me right before a huge day?

She thought, anyways, then she calmly slid into her brown leather satchel. The two split, their friends or phones in hand, tried to peacefully suppress all of the anxiety in the air.

The end of the school day came. Plucked guitar would rain over the evening.

He had made it.

Whether anybody knew what had happened or not. His parents did because they saw a bathtub filled with rope and blood when they got home. Josiah had been sitting on the tiled floor.

He hadn't done it, he almost couldn't (from a moral or purely sympathetic perspective), and his parents let him read a novel in the office room all night afterwards. They did not pester him about any schoolwork or obligations. Further on, they agreed to do away with stressing about the Projects, not even showing up for support so that it didn't seem like a big deal. And it wasn't. And they would definitely ban him from talking to Maralyn anymore. And Rosie, and Jesse, and his more feminine friends at Middleton. They would silently enforce regarding that last group. It was time for him to interact with strong, reputable boys (their example shining onto him), but they didn't want to break his heart, especially after this episode.

As soon as Jay closed the door behind him, at 6 pm, when all three family members home, he thought up all the different scenarios that would go down tomorrow–partly in excitement, partly from sheer anxiety. Even though he had been nearly hospitalized just before, Josiah was relieved and proud about his work. The study room smelled like old gift shop teddy bears, plus an aged candle called "Deep Pine" was lit. The family kept the room in perfect shape, yet he was the only one who ever remembered to enjoy it.

The golden and red curtains slightly parted against the long, narrow panes of glass. Thick but wispy clouds protected his eyes from early summer's harsh sun onset. Before doing what he came here to do, he walked over to the left side wall. He shook the curtains left and right and then peered out. Jay lowered his head slightly, then nervously ruffled his long hair.

The scenery felt peaceful, lost, empowering. The boy's shoulders grew smaller and smaller until he just felt his muddled mind, two numb legs holding it all up. Consciousness and contradictions. This event he was obliged to go to began to crawl about his face, like toxic runoff or a dangerous small insect. But this shock lasted for about three seconds. His dismay was transformed into a more abstract rush. It was like a long tube of pure coldness, a tunnel between him and the object. Whatever this was, it blocked most of his vision, and something internal said to back away from the sun. His skin still absorbed the brisk air of the sterile and ultra air-conditioned room. This predicament mirrored the kid's emotional state of being, of course, or even the other way around. Maybe he created this world. But that was too scary for him. Power. Josiah's camera innocently lied in the shelves by the door. He picked it right up as soon as he (finally) found it and placed his hand on the door knob. He paused there for a minute, flipping through photos with his left hand, and then he left.

The room would get colder since he had left the door open. Later on, the wooden furniture would stop baking and decaying without a powerful evening beam on them. But there was still the moon. And the Projects were tomorrow. That was enough heat and enough sun for the entire Opifer community.

As soon as he heard his parents' voices grow louder, he rushedly packed his backpack with a notebook, pencils, and the camera, then ran to his car. He was going to Maralyn's house to view the final edits–going there for the last time, unknown to her. The notorious Project Creative Portion Videos and Art Galleries would be on display tomorrow.

Chapter 27

Once Katrina walked in and settled in, everybody felt that it was crunch time. This sparkling, shimmering event of light. Their chance to either impress the girl with finality or impress healing upon their shattered hearts. She could have been the medium or the scapegoat. Either way, she was everything. At least to Maralyn.

"Deep," total darkness. Even the darkness glimmered.

A reclusive yet artistically active 10th grader from Sigma turned on his ambient pre-show playlist. Nobody else knew it, but Tim Hecker's vibrant, romantic humming reverberated throughout the room. It smelled good for all, too, the kids' dressed-up attitudes and the girls' anonymous perfumes. The current track was like the bottom of the ocean, and began to scream at one point; the teachers turned their heads to wonder who was playing this nonsense. But the performance would not budge.

What is this, really though? Maralyn thought. She's going to think that this is the cool part, her favorite part, and we haven't even begun.

"Henry!" Trevor projected out, across the entire Opifer main auditorium. Girls turned to him, flashing devious white smiles and mixed intentions turning from bad to loving. "Ay!"

But Henry did not budge while he spoke to Christina and her friends, it seemed as if he ignored it. Devonte clutched onto his red leather satchel, there to contain his cigarettes but also for protection. He glanced up around the room.

A long ten minutes went by. In that time, Rosie had Tweeted, °boyfriend by justin biebes is still a sexy banger and i will not hear otherwise #nojustintimberlake°

What the fuck? Maralyn thought.

Brett responded, °Swag on you°

And her, °OMG lol°–because he even remembered that.

Rosie was seated near Christina, Katrina with her group in between them. The main lights initiated without anybody really noticing, an oscillating cascade of yellow, blue, and pink LED lights from mighty lamps. The school added to and adjusted the lighting rig a few weeks before every Project Video day. Part of Maralyn's inspiration and knowledge about art lighting came from, rebelliously, playing around in this room with Dakota, Trevor, and Brett. Josiah was never there, though; the one time he was, the fun boys left early. The boy backstage, Webster, set the lights to swirl about, mainly resting on the stage up and down. Yellow became clear as the base color. The floor had two green lamps swirling on it.

It was still too dark to move around normally, but faces could be seen better as this yellow and green persisted. Katrina's eyes seemed more hooded than they were, pure white beaming from inside. In the next track, Ben Frost's rattling basses innerved the space from the top down. Contrasting with music's tendency to send bass to the ground first.

Several 30 and 40-something "Directors" floating around, the space still reeked of high school, no matter how potent the good spirits. Of extra jobs and overdue bills. Anyhow, Sage's softspoken mother and father descended three rows to sit by Dakota's mom and Jesse's parents. Grade school parents were always confident, and the ones to be obeyed. Perhaps they were the real ones enrolled. One more, long, ambient slash noise song pursued the audience's hearts and the Project Videos began.

Clink. All black. Mr. Allen sat in the front row all the way to the left.

The first piece saw a girl trio from Sigma–Sigma students often opened up for the evening–singing Britney Spears' "Lucky."

They were aware of how much both their looks and personalities conformed to this, but they circumvented criticism with their hard-worked art. Their new title was "Money." They had relayered the melody to concoct a simple acapella track, using vocals in the place of drums and synth. The lyrics were altered, the chorus going:

"She loves money, he's a star
But they cry, cry, cry in their lonely heart thinking
If there's nothing missing in their lives
Then why do those tears come at night?"

Mostly everyone thought that the cute video was at least interesting, the teachers giving a clean round of applause for them. Josiah and Maralyn, mainly the latter, were worried about how their video would appear shown so closely to something like this.

Soon, this phase of Projects was over. Several Sigma videos had been shown, including Trevor, Elisa, and their friend's–and now a five minute break. Next, a few videos from Middleton students.

Maralyn sat in that auditorium anxious but feeling lights on her. Feeling a cold hole inside of her. She opened her phone. She quickly opened Twitter, then scrolled through dozens of lines, images, videos, links. There were Van Gogh paintings, Egyptian artifacts, news of journalists' slayings, old Donald Trump Tweets, next to memes about Britney Spears, Facebook culture, college. Her insides were a mosaic of confusion, excitement, despair, jolliness, anxiety, and pure energy. And dozens, hundreds, thousands, millions, billions of kids around her were doing the same. Her crouched back hid agonized, wide eyes–all of her focus concentrated to the device.

She did look up when she heard a group, sounding like Rosie and Trevor, laugh while passing around a meme on a phone. It pleasured her to see this, smiling.

Then, she decided to message her mother. It was impulsive, almost sporadic, but still love-based. Of course, it was to her mother. She crunched her hungover eyes and pressed iMessage open.

She noticed texts already from her: °Love u so much° with a flower and a plant emoji. °Picking you up at 10?°

At them, her smile emanated the strength warmth of her day.

It seemed to come by quicker than she expected or liked, but it was time for Katrina, Henry, and Benny's video. Trevor had left the group to join Elisa and another boy from Sigma. Their video was shown an hour b

The scene was lit up with green and purple laser lines and shadows created by the dust, and above all was the title of their video, in bold blue Times New Roman letters: A Grey Horizon Came For Me When All I Knew Was Sun

Lyrics about running away from a loved one and expressing guilt over mistakes made with them were entrenched in Katrina's head then. In the foreground, a dark electronic beat spun like spiders finishing a large web. Her consciousness expressed not embarrassment, guilt, or shame–only purity.

When Maralyn stared up at that line, she thought to herself: it should rather be "Karma Came For Me When We Were At Our Best" or "But It Wasn't Our Fault." And the anxiety began to trickle down her ribs. Her cotton t-shirt would be wet by thirty seconds into the video.

It was just anxiety's thing.

A low sound quality guitar began to strum after an interval of blackness. The chords were hard to discern, but distinguishable–in the style of indie music à la mode, and Henry began singing. He wore a soft-looking red flannel and sadly looked into the camera. It was a simple cover of "Who Loves The Sun" by The Velvet Underground. The song was the closest her group found to expressing their feelings, without actually making a new song.

There were sporadic VHS shots of single flowers, pavement, and smoking chimneys. Almost every student checked their phones at some point, some stretching it for minutes on end. They seemed like compulsive, anxious actions.

All of the boys there blushed when a dimly lit side profile of Katrina came into view. She glared up, at what seemed like a sun which wasn't there, as Henry's ethereal crying sounded. She peered, warriors inside of her mindfield seething against death itself.

The video finished quickly to Maralyn. When it did, mainly only the teachers clapped. The kids gently smiled at Katrina and Trevor–although he had not worked on it. Some crawled over to pat the girl on the back. She gave back a contented smile, not letting them see her bright teeth. And then she peered at the door.

No, don't leave, Maralyn thought with intensity.

It seemed to work, because Katrina slouched back into her seat. She nestled into her dim phone screen.

"Alrightie! Time for Josiah and Maralyn's video." Mr. Allen's voiced projected in his microphone.

Jesus christ, Maralyn thought.

Utter silence commenced.

"It is," he paused, to bring the cue card closer to his face, "called 'Below Ground Energies.' Alright, go ahead up there and play it. I've known these two kids for a long time and can only I encourage you in the rest of your careers, Maralyn in your photography and directorship and Josiah in your piano and…modeling."

The room laughed, even though they didn't know understand the joke (yet). Maralyn realized that she was eternally grateful to the teacher. Webster hit play.

Beginning: black. Two white flashes, then a lasting orange screen.

"Waahhh!" was the opening vocal; edited to not be too overpowering or startling for the intended audience.

It accompanied a clean electric guitar melody, flowing in. And then cuts of their beat began.

Darkened and blurry images of light.

32 seconds in, each element stabilized; the guitar strummed up and down and the beat felt like slowed down old hip hop. The camera faded into Josiah in a large pink shirt and super baggy, dark jeans. He spun around with his arms outstretched. The artificial-looking blonde wig, which they had argued about, flowed beautifully from the wind and movements. His soft Asian skin seemed tanner than in real life. Grey clouds overhead. He growled:

"We all only know
How to hurt each other
But I found love in the hate
I saw love through the pain"

His voice sounded youthful, but confident in ultimate.

Then, Josiah began his rap verse cascade, also known as "spazzing out." He appeared to be shouting into the camera, on top of a parking garage:

"What do you want from me? (Huh?)
Front on me? Step on me? (Ouch!)
17 million like my years, 0 for the coat because I go no dollars
Whipping it with B and J but I'm just tryna find inner peace
And there's nowhere to go
Yuh!
There's a master and an assignment but we keep it 3 easy
No sacrilege or martyrs (beeh!)
Just M&Ms waiting to be piled (grr)
Because I'm a good person
And this is what good people do
YO"

"3 easy" referred to the Holy Trinity, which had annoyed Maralyn because probably no one would understand it, but Josiah knew that people would find it cool. And they did. Much came to execution, plus some (like Katrina and Mr. Allen) immediately felt a special message behind it. K also liked it because it reminded her of the artist André 3000. Josiah's "yo" interjection was a double entendre: it took the place of "hoe" and also jokingly referred to his Chinese origins. Maralyn shook her head and smiled every time.

The rest of the song resumed via the instrumental loudening. Josiah bounced around. Maralyn had not inserted any transitions here, only following him in a dizzying circle.

Their friends' eyes were smiling; Katrina smirked.

"We all only know
How to hurt each other
But I found love in the hate
I saw love through the pain"

Good peach, bad peach
I eat mud and dirt for fun
Mud and dirt for fun…
Cancer and getting better grades
Yuh"

The shots during the conclusion of the video panned to Jay's face, showing a wink and then a single tear streaming. The colors turned black and white, and then a white flash, and then a black one, and then a slow alternation of the two. During this, shoegaze influences became apparent with the his voice reduced to a mutter, the guitar sounding like someone had their two feet on it. Maralyn saw Jim Morrison's face.

"Oh, you were such a special friend to me
Not like my parents
Not like my dad
(Gross!)"

Most of these words were indecipherable. They almost had to be; Josiah was singing about something homosexual. And disrespecting one's parents would probably garner bad rep from those doing the grading. The screen turned orange, then navy blue, then a final yellow when all the drums stripped away. Green borders.

Oh, she thought, I feel it real now. Wallah,

The look on Katrina's face seemed genuine like coffee beans, like she was astounded at the turns of Maralyn's overflowing mind.

Silently now, slowly, she got to communicate delicacies and volcanoes. Still in her crush daze, which was apparent to some people there.

I want to make her feel like this, Maralyn thought, I want to make her experience this for the rest of my life–

The yellow video stopped. It ended, it was over. The pair's entire Project work was over, they'd only have to submit their grades and essay questions to colleges. They would have to close their invisible glass and microphones, stifle the addictive social cues between those they have known for years. Hopefully, tonight was at least sensational. For all.

Well, that was lazy, Mrs. Millington thought. But even she appeared joyful–this was a big event, even for her "artsy partsy" kids.

Sage's solo video, a courageous endeavor, was up next. Afterwards, everyone would head home, or if they were like Maralyn's friends, have a party.

A minute went by, everyone who had been in his friend group shuffled in their seats a little bit uncomfortably. "Had" because the group had broken apart. Heather said the other day, "Nobody even goes to the lot, anymore." He actually was still friends with most, if not all, of them–having mainly excluded those who took to black culture too much (which included Brett, Rosie, and somewhat both Katrina and Maralyn). He only still spoke to the latter two because they were cute and consistently kind to him.

"Okay, once everyone politely shuts up we will commence the strong and intelligent Sage's video," The crowd laughed. "Plus it's a solo one, so get ready!"

A hip hop beat began to pour in via the surround sound speakers. There was a light bass presence, which could be felt more in the back of the auditorium, as well as several uniquely layered taps.

Did he produce this? Trevor thought. That's so dope,

The electronic piano hills matched the quiet snares, all while his video showed. It was landscape-based, with self-made filters or animations appearing intermittently. One of these was a straight lightning bolt stretching the length of the screen. Mountains, captured by simply his iPhone, from across Sage's March roadtrip soared by. The cutaway shots were one of many elements that he had studied over the months. His filters were created by projecting red or green lasers, borrowed at a local theatre, onto a black backdrop and the lens itself. There was also a sequence where a plastic Greek sculpture head, which his friend Khayrah had made for her Project, became enveloped by the effects of a purple lamp and a smoke machine.

It was a generally peaceful and calm film, with provocative effects on the body. Mostly everybody clapped when it was over, and videos from two groups that Maralyn knew were next. There were several in total left, but her and her friends would leave instead.

Chapter 28

They made it to their underground spot.

Their sneakers or leather shoes made a neat circle in a muddy, leaf-filled region. The dirt was inescapable at corners, the rest of the ground covered in something whitish blue–like mold or old paint. The place appeared as disgusting as it always did, but those wet, cooler colors in the night added a heavenliness. It was by an abandoned Opifer parking lot, lower in earth than the main one and near the middle school elevators.

Maralyn adjusted her eye makeup with a tiny mirror. It was hard to see and she felt stupid, so she put it away, even knowing that her mascara was probably smeared. Would anyone tell her if so? She trusted at least Jesse the most at that point, and had Rosie there too but that girl had begun revolving around others too much.

A radiator gave off a soft wind, pronounced by a subtle buzzing sound. It beeped every 5 minutes, which was relatively loud in the lowkey situation and unsettling them at first.

Trevor thought that it preceded a hidden door opening. He got so fearful that he was close to retreating entirely. The kids efficiently told him off, though, saying not to worry while laughing at him.

Maralyn had realized at home that day that even if their showing was a complete flop, no teachers wanted to recognize their will to innovation. Alchemy and lifebuilding. And if her friends didn't like it, somebody hated on it, everybody else found it weird. The usual path would still be laid out. She would go home, look at Jim Morrison, and pick up her camera again.

I guess I have to keep striving for labors of love, she thought.

Her mind could even be stable enough to churn out equal if not better results.

"Here!" Trevor nearly shouted, poking his vape mod towards Henry. "Here, fucking here you go,"

Dakota and Rosie smirked. Trevor had basically just licensed the entire group to take hits from it. And while they were doing that, Maralyn simply continued to reflect. She made a point to herself that she would stick to these resolutions. She would at least try to.

"Green"

The next day, Sunday.

Maralyn called Josiah because she was confused, almost offended, that he did not hang out with the ol' group, as well as ghosted her. Right before and then after the showings.

"What the fuck, dude?" she asked angrily.

She was on the verge of tears.

"Um," he blankly responded. After a moment, barely serious, "Well I hope you had fun,"

"Gee, thanks," she answered. "I did. And where were you? Are we even friends anymore?"

"Maralyn, Maralyn," he deadly responded. Slightly exasperated, trying to hang up soon in order to combat that, "Don't even…act like you care, anymore. You don't give a fuck about this friendship,"

She gasped audibly. Her parents and Elias were yelling downstairs, her usual call to put everything down and join them. And she did not want to, but she felt compelled like she almost deserved it.

"I don't understand. I don't even know what to say," she told Josiah. "All I do is care for you and help you with stuff. People loved our video, why were you so…not into it?"

"Or…anything?" she added quietly. Fearful of his reaction. Fearful of vulnerability. Fearful of trust.

He chuckled into the phone.

"You honestly don't seem to get anything,"

To Maralyn, this person sounded like somebody suddenly being controlled by robots. It was not her Josiah.

"You just kind of, Maralyn, you just love! to! get! attention! And talk about the same people and do the same things and never really improve or change. And so I think we can't talk that much anymore, because, we just have different priorities in life! And that's fine. Just like, please get your life together, and then talk to me,"

He sounded securely nervous, as if unsure about the entire future except his own.

Maralyn didn't have to say anything to suggest that he had made her speechless, it was audible with her hesitations and the phone muffling. A few moments went by.

"Well," she told him.

"Yeah,"

"Yeah,"

And another silence.

Then, "Welp, yeah; the world is really fucked right now. And the political climate is really bad, and we all just need to sit and heal, and leave each other alone, and then maybe…we'll figure things out. I don't know, Maralyn. Maybe,"

"Yeah," she replied. "Maybe."

Geez, I'm sorry, she wanted to say.

After some useless small talk, to end things with remote normalcy, Josiah quickly ended the phone call. Their conversation had seemed short, like there would be more to this. If not soon, then later. Or maybe Maralyn was wishful thinking.

Now.

Alone. Covered in her depression.

She remembered Kurt now, and seemingly only his hand, as if they had held hands on that day.

Oh yeah, she thought, remembering the school shooting, which was so close to home. She reflected on the horror–with no shock, no surprise.

Zero feeling.

Chapter 29

Finally back to school; Monday.

The second to last week of school.

It was a travesty in itself that the tragedy occurred so late in the year. The students today were heavily desensitized. This was evident in that few from the middle and high schools brought up the situation, and select groups discussed it on social media. Those were liberals or kids mad at the world. Yet, there were some clashes, despite the overall numbness–Maralyn's group did all it could to avoid those.

Saturday was on for rolling Bubba Kush backwoods and playing "Dazed and Confused" with Heather's projector in her basement.

As announced overhead to the entire school, there would be a moment of silence after lunchtime and a roundtable discussion about gun violence sometime tomorrow. The latter would be hosted by the Nonpartisan Politics Club from Middleton–not a surprise as most Sigma students were Republican and advocated gun ownership. Or at least their parents were. There were no interesting animals in Opifer's area, besides deer, but they insisted that citizens should own military-style guns (especially in reference to that wording in the Second Amendment). Whether their political affiliations connected to this primitive display of patriotism was unclear.

Lunch went by, the moment of silence occurred (several students could not sit still), and a popular alternative artist announced a tour.

"What's up?" Rosie asked Maralyn when they met after second period. She was trying to invite her to a gathering in the evening.

"Nothing much, what's good," she answered. "Just playing Kodak Black in my ears,"

She chuckled. "Good stuff."

They both looked out at the kids rushing from and to class, sentimentally bothered. Brett ran past at one point, hands shoved into his jean pockets.

"Well anyways," Rosie said. They laughed. "Do you want to come over tonight?"

"Yes, yeah sure," Maralyn told her. "To do what?"

"I don't know, listen to Jesse's new recordings or something. We'll have food, though," she said with smiling eyes.

Maralyn told her she'd be there. They ran off to their next classes.

At the End of the Day

Henry was at the house, and was playing fresh alternative rap music for Jordan, the photography kid. He had invited him after getting the okay from Rosie. Tangerine peels were on the table in front of them, plus Henry's vape that neither had touched so far. Jordan's head bobbed to a song by lil tracy.

Maralyn arrived, having resorted to walking the 20 minutes because she was sick of driving with her parents or friends in breaking relationships. Really, these rides were no longer available. She knocked the door, not text her, to make Rosie laugh.

Rosie seemed out of breath and even sweaty. She said from behind the glass screen door, "Hi! How are you? I'm already a Jehovah's Witness, I'm sorry,"

"Jesus fucking christ, just open the door."

"Yeah, I'm going to have to talk to my mom and dad first. Can you hold?"

"Rosie, I will kill myself right here and now."

"Yeah, I don't know about that. Thank you so much, though!" she replied. "I appreciate all of your offers! Do you have the cookies? Where are the cookies?"

Maralyn proceeded to opening the door herself, saying to her giggling friend, "The cookies are up my ass,"

She ignored Henry and Jordan were unusually close together, ignored the paraphernalia, ignored a Kanye West interview playing on the Apple TV. She didn't know what she was doing. She felt where she had to go. And she walked there.

Navy and baby blue stars seemed to be at the top of her black perception.

She got to Rosie's room. It smelled of cigarette smoke hosted on clothing. Her metaphysical ears perked.

Maralyn walked through the half-open door. An instant breath of relief. Katrina had been sitting on the bed on her phone–unusual for her–red face. She stood up. She took Maralyn's hands and looked into her eyes for a few moments. She looked at her straightly.

And Maralyn, both really, experienced feeling, forgiveness, joy, hope. Katrina sighed in relief while pulling away from their hug after that. And she had thought about the kids who had lost their lives while they did, sending a neutral prayer to them all.

Virtue, light. Strength and God.

Maralyn understood now; she got it.

They quietly parted ways–in peace, in something.

There, that evening, she wanted to play Kid Cudi for everyone–but maybe another day would do. Everybody was distracting themselves with songs and memes and lovers.

When her mom texted her that she was on her way, at 10pm and after much vaping, Maralyn stood near the door. She simply looked down. Katrina and Rosie were on the couch.

Katrina rose–towards her complicated, not broken or breaking anymore, friend.

The wide but not tall platform was destroyed–showing only the kids floating. Then Jesse's vocals reverberated. Her singing something which sounded like the letter "a" was clearest. A spiky star against a black space flashed.

"How are you?" Katrina asked, looking to Maralyn's hands.

Maralyn was wordless, but she said, "I'm alright. I have to go soon, though."

Katrina nodded, her head downward.

"I'll see you again," she told Maralyn.

"Yeah," she replied sweetly, breathily. "Of course,"

And the girl was soon picked up. The scent on her clothes was not masked well, but her mother did not care today.

"I'm just tryna keep my cool.
Prescriptions change my attitude
And my heart can't take this altitude."
–Lil Zubin - Overdose (feat. Wicca Phase Springs Eternal)

When she got home, Maralyn immediately texted Katrina.

Because pure silence was not enough; there was a need for words. And she also could not contain the feeling, the moment.

°Listen°

Katrina immediately replied: °hello.°

°If you don't know anything else, just know that i love you° °however it is, however we'll be. I'll try to be there for you°

°And I'm really glad i got that letter to you, im glad it worked out° Maralyn added, originally having wanted to say "it worked."

°yes, you just keep doing your thing. ill do mine too.. just stay focused on your goals and all those things°

°and thank you for your nice words. it means a lot. we dont completely know what each other has been thru, which can be really tough when trying to be friends or close at all°

°I completely agree. I didn't know who i was before, but I think I know now :)°

°yeah, i think i know more about myself now too. you helped me with that°

°so thank you°

°you write beautifully !°

Maralyn felt as if a great, snowy mountain, against a crisp river, had grown inside of her.

°Wow, why thank you° And °!° she added a few seconds later, fearful that her other would quit the conversation.

°yuh huh, buddy°

Maralyn wanted to reply °Hahaha° but did not want to ruin the mood. She unthinkingly sent, instead, °:))°

°and i liked what you said at then end° Katrina sent.

In an effort to seem interesting, Maralyn waited a minute before responding. She replied, °Oh word? Good 2 know°

°...°

°maybe one day it could work between us, who knows . if we're bored°

M backed away at this and realized that she was falling into her phone. Her head was leaning forward, her eyeballs nearly touching the screen. She felt that of course this wasn't healthy, looked away for a few moments, then laughed at herself. While typing, her mind, or perhaps her soul, brought back feelings of rosemary oil and outer space.

She said, °Trust. I <3 you°

°I've honestly had this letter mostly written for a while, I was just never sure when to give it to you or how. But I wrote the final version and just had to let go°

°And I'm glad i gave it to you, and now, at this point in the world. I °

Katrina responded, °tru°

°I had this other letter written which I have saved and kinda wanna burn, it was more angry, and I dont wanna show you or anyone°

°oh damn, lol° Katrina sent after a solemn pause. She began to hear the loud ruffling down the hall, but ignored everything.

Maralyn returned with the following, in excited bursts, °It was just at a super crappy and weird/confusing time of this year, and it was full of straight bullshit and criticizing stuff and bringing back bad old memories. Just not a pretty perspective, especially moving forward..°

°Anyways, do you want to get gourmet smoothies with me sometime?°

°We can Netflix and smoothies like good, civilized grrls do°

°;) maybe° the girl replied.

She has a lot of work to do, Katrina thought while chuckling, she doesn't know how much I hate smoothies or cold things,

President Relevant Society My Shmevelant

Climbing. Climbing the black star. Strength, full force, and flexing of the left hand, and then right. Radiation down and up both of the arms, the same arms, and burying the face within a textbook. Breathing in the ink, dead trees, dead paper, dead money, dead Presidents, real Presidents, office casual business forms–pantsuits, tracksuits, forms, boys and women and death and tall trees and eastern or western success.

Deep, deep success.

Climbing, soaring–the sound of wind gushing ruptures their eardrums. Climbing, the icebreaker. They're, not her, not hers, not theirs. It's always they, it's always they're. Bashing, bashful.

I had found you here, Maralyn thought, while she visited the screen world for the last time.

She swore on it, promising to herself, her little brother, and the ethereal boy from the library that she would roam the healthier route of living in space and taking in time and understanding and experiencing life.

But now I know where you are, where you really are–she thought–and it wasn't meant to be like this,

Bass. The hill. Dying.

"We died." Congratulations, you're free now. "We failed and you meant it."

Like an outsider shadow: How long did it take you to make it here? What stopped you?

Homophobes. Penis. Vagina.

How many hours did you kill first? In boredom? In spite? In bloom?

Rap, bass music, rap. You meant every word, for me, to me, Jesus Christ on the cross–our President meant every word, our teacher only speaks the truth and that's why they're successful.

النهاية

About the Author

Lyan Alsabti is a writer, artist, and student based out of Metro Detroit, Michigan. As of this book's release, she attends Wayne State University and works with the Ascension St. John Health System. She is interested in philosophical perspectives on healing, pop culture, and human nature.

She can be reached at the following social media handles:

Twitter: @lyan_alsab

Instagram: @gf2a.novel

or this email: gf2aofficial@gmail.com

31891474R00126

Made in the USA
Columbia, SC
11 November 2018